# Isobella

# ISOBELLA

Margaret Nyhon

Willow Press
Otago, New Zealand

*Isobella — such a beautiful name,*
*sadly you didn't do it justice,*
*you brought it shame.*

*There was a moment in time when the tide*
*turned,*
*but even from this, you didn't learn.*

*For one moment in time the tide turned,*
*but even from this,*
*you didn't learn.*

# 1

# Isobella, Why Art Thou So Wicked?

Today was Isobella's father's funeral. It was sad that Bartholomew had left his family, but in truth, it was his time to pass on. He had never really recovered from his operation, but he was not young any more, in fact he was eighty-seven years old. The place he was going to would be a welcome peace for him, away from all the arguments. Now poor little Bobo the dog would have to bear the brunt of his wife's alcohol-fuelled anger.

Isobella's mother, Matilda, was far from easygoing on her poor husband. He could not understand why she had to indulge in consuming alcohol, especially when he was so against it. There was no give or take from either party on this issue, so it was an ongoing war, a battle that had been raging for many years. Only now could it be laid to rest, because at last Matilda was a free woman. Bartholomew was no longer going to rule her life, he was gone.

Matilda sat in her old chair and gazed into space. She was reminiscing about her past, remembering one incident in particular, one that her husband and children thought was funny, but she could find no humour in it at all ... She had arrived home very late one evening to find she had been locked out so she called out to Bartholomew but to no avail. She went out to her vegetable patch and lay on the ground among the potatoes and drifted off to sleep. Many hours later she awoke feeling cold water soaking her. Her husband had found her asleep in the garden and turned the sprinkler on.

To the outside world Matilda looked sad, on this her husband's burial day, but deep down she was quietly relieved, because now she could live the rest of her life her way. Not that her life was the norm. The mourners were gathering, as were two of Matilda's children, James and Isobella, and James's children. Jessica was living in London and could not make it home for the funeral.

But it was Isobella's entrance that turned heads. One could have been forgiven in thinking that she had arrived for a red-carpet event instead of her father's funeral. Her white see-through top outlined her well-endowed breasts, her white trousers looked like they were painted on and her stilettos were nearly as high as Mt Everest. She was the pinnacle of fashion, but why today? Today belonged to her father; why take the attention from him and make this her day? But this was Isobella.

Matilda was visibly shaken by her daughter's choice

of dress, on this day of mourning, as were other family members. Although Matilda asked Isobella to change into something more respectable she pretended not to hear this, so the request fell on deaf ears, as it always did with Isobella; like mother, like daughter.

Isobella was self-centred and spoilt. She was spoilt rotten right from the moment she entered this world. She was born a princess in her mother and father's eyes, and she grew up believing this was her standing in life. She deserved to be spoilt, life owed it to her.

She was the middle child. Jessica was born two years after Isobella but she did not receive the same attention that was bestowed on her older sister. James their brother was older than his sisters. He was born while his father was at war and he was four years old when Bartholomew returned home. He had another father figure in his life and that was his grandfather, whom he knew and loved. James felt safe with his grandfather and grandmother, this is where he was loved most. To have a stranger walk into his life was traumatic for a four-year-old.

The girls on the other hand were post-war babies. Isobella was totally adored by her parents, especially her father; she was his little princess. The bond was there from the moment he held her in his arms. He did not experience this with James. Matilda wanted a beautiful name for her eldest daughter. She was not happy with her own name as it was plain; she was high-end fashion, but the name Matilda certainly was not. Isobella had a lovely tone to it, it was classy and everyone would remember this name, and the person it belonged to ... oh how true.

The church was filling with mourners. Relations had come from near and far to say their goodbyes to this law-abiding citizen who belonged to many local organisations. He was an upstanding man in the community.

The family were seated in the front pews in the local Catholic church. This would be a first in a very long time, as the family only attended or used the church for weddings or funerals, never for religious beliefs. Therefore, they were not a practising Catholic family, but when needed the church was there.

The service began with a welcome to everyone by the local priest, then the following: "We are all gathered here today to farewell Bartholomew Joseph O'Brien who was a loving husband and father to his family ...," followed by all the necessary paraphernalia that happened at a good Catholic funeral. As the service drew to a close, the pallbearers were requested to come forward and carry Bartholomew to his final resting place. And there, as the first pallbearer, was the most important person, Isobella, and next to her stood James, but it was Isobella who stole the limelight.

All eyes were fixed on this fashion icon as she haughtily tossed her head in the air and took up the first position at the head of the coffin. This was *her* father, never mind James, he hardly deserved a mention. Sadly Bartholomew had been outstaged by his darling Isobella. She had stolen his last hours of glory!

The whispers and sneers that went around the congregation centred on one person. She had made the statement that she had come to make, that was to validate her position as 'Daddy's little princess'. Matilda was disheartened by the show of utter disrespect by her daughter, but this would just be passed over, as it always was. Even the most blatant lies and torrid behaviour was always either forgiven or forgotten. But not this time, especially by family members; they would not let this lay to rest, as it was them that had to carry the embarrassment.

Matilda couldn't wait for this all to be over; she needed a little pick-me-up, sooner rather than later.

The after-function was held at the church hall and people began to gather there after leaving the cemetery. James and his wife, Lillian, and their two children, Brad and Amelia, with their respective families, along with relatives and friends, all met to discuss the day's events. This was the last time they could say their final farewells, but of course the conversation veered away from Bartholomew, guess who to? Isobella!

Bartholomew had been a successful businessman and was in partnership in several business premises in this thriving seaside town. Even the city mayor had come to pay his respects, as he had met Bartholomew on many occasions at business meetings, and found him to be an upstanding citizen.

Amelia was the first to voice her opinion. "Aunty Isobella went even further down in my estimation today, fancy wearing such inappropriate clothes to Grandie's funeral, I will never forgive her."

Then of course outspoken Brad endorsed his sister's words. "Isobella is a self-opinionated witch; who was she trying to impress? I don't even want people to know she is my aunty."

This pretty well summed up the feelings of her brother James's family.

As Lillian looked around the room, there sitting at a table with a few friends was her sister-in-law Isobella. There was no love lost between these two women; it wasn't that she totally disliked Isobella, but she could not understand why she showed so much resentment towards

James — he was her brother. She showed no love or respect for him, and very little for Jessica. Isobella was the one who won their parents' affection; why be like this with James? Lillian came from a loving family, and could not understand why a family with three siblings barely spoke to each other. But the wedge had been there for many years, put in place by their parents, as Isobella was the spoilt princess whose every demand was obeyed, otherwise people suffered.

Several weeks had now passed since the funeral and Matilda had her house and her life back in order. Bartholomew had left her well off with his commercial buildings and other small holdings, all of which he had gone in with partners. He had also provided for his favourite daughter Isobella in his will, leaving her a tidy sum to help make her life a little easier. He hoped she would make good use of the money.

James was not provided for as he had worked hard and set himself up, he did not need any money, in his father's eyes. He would get a third share of what was left after Matilda had passed away. Isobella just needed a little boost in the meantime, and because Jessica lived in London she was more or less forgotten.

Bartholomew was gone, the arguing was over and Bobo was thoroughly spoilt; he didn't argue with Matilda, she could drink as much as she pleased, Bobo didn't mind. This was the life that Matilda longed for.

She didn't have to be home at any given time as there was no Bartholomew to cook for. She could now drink as she pleased because this was her home, so out came the bottles from their hidden stashes, that era was done and dusted. No more of her booty would have to be emptied down the sink, then followed by battle number ... whatever.

On one of James and Lillian's visits to see how Matilda was coping without Bartholomew, they noticed a lovely bunch of red roses in a vase on her table. They were definitely from a florist, one knew this because of the lovely ribbons flowing from the flowers, it had a professional touch to it.

Lillian jokingly said to her mother-in-law, "Oh, it didn't take you long to find a new admirer." With this Matilda answered, "This is a long story, but not today." But deep in Lillian's heart she sensed one day Matilda would explain the flowers to her, but this was not the right moment. They had a good relationship.

Matilda liked her daughter-in-law, as she was a kind-hearted person, who genuinely cared for her. She was the total opposite to Isobella, who was selfish, mean and spiteful. Matilda often expressed her deep disappointment with Isobella, but really, she had no one else to blame other than herself. Whether she knew this was another matter!

But like mother, like daughter, they both had the looks to die for, they were as two peas in a pod. Unless you fitted into the 'beautiful people' criteria you didn't amount to much in their eyes. Their lives revolved around the skin-deep perception that as long as you looked the part, then that was all that mattered. What was lurking underneath was not an issue, because that could not be seen. Matilda dressed young for her age, but always looked beautiful, with jewellery adorning her neckline, perhaps to hide the double chin that had unwantedly appeared. Isobella, on the other hand, had a figure that would make a sack look glamorous, and this she knew, along with her plunging necklines, and short hemlines. Her olive skin and brunette hair just added more colour to her picture. But behind this façade was a jealous, self-centred person who did not take kindly to her mother's friendship with Lillian.

No one was ever good enough for Isobella, she soon tired of people and things — they just became her cast-offs. She had become the 'femme fatale spider' who spun her web, trapping all vulnerable prey. In the middle of her web was a young lad who had been on the scene for quite some time, but at what capacity was anyone's guess. Was he a boarder? But as time passed, he became her constant companion, and it was now apparent to all that Isobella had acquired a 'toy boy'. Whether true or not was another matter!

An admission from Matilda to Lillian one evening after having a couple of wines left her feeling a little uncomfortable. "I can't understand why my good-looking children married such plain partners. Isobella was so beautiful she could have had anyone she wanted. Instead she ended up with plain old Jeffrey."

This was a rebellious act by Isobella to prove she could make her own decisions. Her parents, especially Matilda, were not impressed. Matilda had much bigger expectations of Isobella and she felt her beauty was wasted on Jeffrey. There were far more deserving men out there for her daughter. She had never met Jessica's husband as he was an Englishman. "And James had some stunning girlfriends, his last one was lovely, but then you came along."

If Lillian had not been a grounded sort of person, then this would have hurt her, but she knew the fickle nature of her mother-in-law. "Now is the right time to tell you about the roses you spied on my table a few weeks after the funeral."

It was as if Bartholomew had been forgotten already.

"They were a gift from the city mayor for Isobella." Lillian was taken aback, in fact shocked. She had not expected this explanation. "Why would he be sending flowers to Isobella, he is a married man?" It was in this moment in time that Lillian learnt an affair had begun between Isobella and the city mayor. The femme fatale spider had spun another victim into her web. The see-through top and the slinky pants did have a part to play at Bartholomew's funeral, but for all the wrong reasons.

How could this happen? Here was a man who was well known in the community, but worse than that, he was accompanied by his wife to many public outings and business functions. At this stage, she would not have suspected that her husband was cheating on her; how would she react if she knew? But then no one knew, even Lillian would not have known if Matilda had not consumed that extra glass of wine. How was she going to tell James? He would be devastated and totally embarrassed by his sister's latest shenanigans.

The big question! How long would it be before this scandal hit town, was it going to wash in quietly or would it hit in the form of a tsunami? What action would Isobella's toy boy take, as he was a hot-headed young lad? So many questions!

# 2

# Looking Back

Isobella's life had been full of drama. She had met a businessman after leaving her husband; he was her ideal partner, good looking, a natty dresser, and very pleasant. He was very popular. They both had a liking for clothes, both dressed immaculately, they were the beautiful people. Matilda was happy with this match, because at last Isobella had found a good-looking guy. They flittered here and there, spent up large and enjoyed life. There were no worries about tomorrow, because tomorrow would take care of itself.

But sadly, tomorrow did arrive. The old jealousy started to creep in. Who was he with, where was he? Suddenly Anthony was being stalked by Isobella; she wanted to know his every movement, but with his job this was not possible. If he wasn't home when she thought he should be, she would jump into her car and start searching for him. When the slightest bit of suspicion surfaced in Isobella's mind, she went into revenge mode.

It was not uncommon for Anthony to pull up the driveway, and there to greet him were his shirts, lying on the lawn with all the buttons cut off. When Isobella was really, really mad the shirt sleeves were gone. So began a rollercoaster relationship that was going to rise and fall due to Isobella's jealousy.

Then one day the unimaginable happened. Anthony was badly hurt in a car crash. He lay in the city hospital for several weeks in an induced coma, until the doctors could ascertain what damage was done. This meant no income, and with no savings to fall back on, how were they going to survive? Isobella had to swallow her pride and get a job as a waitress, then work out how she was going to get her life sorted.

One day out of the blue Lillian received a phone call from Isobella; it was a cry for help. For what other reason would she want to make contact? She asked for James but he was away. "Lillian, I need some money, I am behind with my rent and I have to go to the city. Anthony has had another seizure, so I want to be with him. The hospital rang, they want me to come down." How could Lillian refuse? This was her sister-in-law asking for help. She rang her and James's bank manager, and asked him to withdraw some money from their joint account and put it in an envelope. It would be picked up shortly by Isobella.

That was the last contact Isobella had with Lillian and James for some time. They only met occasionally when their visits to Matilda's clashed. Months went by and Anthony's health was deteriorating. Since he had been brought out of the induced coma, there had not been the progress the doctors had hoped for. He was much worse than everyone feared. There was little that could be done, it was a matter of waiting to see if he improved. He had been badly crushed, and had severe internal injuries.

The day came when Anthony passed away. This left Isobella with no money, other than what she earned, and nowhere to live. So much for the flitting around while things were good. To Isobella, life was there to enjoy, and money was there to be spent. Next week there would be another pay packet.

Isobella's next ask became a problem, one that Bartholomew could not solve on his own. She had found a home she liked and wanted to buy, but of course had no money. Isobella approached her father to see if he would help her out, but he had to go to his bank and get a loan. His bank turned him down, citing that he was too old to get a loan and be guarantor, and that he had to consider Matilda and his own future. Isobella's credit rating at the bank didn't exactly help her gain any brownie points. Bartholomew approached his partners but none of them would agree to mortgage any of the buildings. Next, of course, there was James.

James received a visit from his father asking if he would arrange a loan at his bank, so his sister could buy the house she just had to have. The bond between father and son had never advanced beyond being cordial to each other, simply because James was pushed aside so that Isobella could have everything in life that she desired. James's mind went back in time to a particular incident that he had never forgiven his father for. He was standing in front of the open fire trying to get warm, as he had been outside chopping firewood in the freezing cold, when Isobella entered the room and demanded to have the fire. Bartholomew told

James to move away so his sister could warm herself. This was only one of many incidents that James had to endure.

Now he was expected to support his sister. James spoke with Lillian to see how she felt. Together they agreed that it was the right thing to do, so the next day James went to his bank and arranged a loan for Isobella so she could buy the house that she just had to have. This was only made possible by James's standing at the bank and his backing. Now Isobella was the proud owner of her own home, something she deserved, even if not one penny came from her own pocket. Hopefully she would always remember how she came to own it. One would have to wait and see!

# 3

# The Continuing Saga

A tsunami had hit the town. The townspeople left their homes rushing here and there spreading the latest scandal. "Have you heard about the city mayor? He is having an affair, his poor wife, who is this 'other woman'?"

In the hotel door blew the gossip. It swirled around the tables like a whirlwind. Matilda had popped in to have a well-deserved drink just for no reason, when it settled at her table. "Matilda, the city mayor is having an affair; do you know who the other woman is?" On hearing this she nearly choked on her final sips. The wine did not slip down easy, instead it lodged in her windpipe. "I have to go!" she yelled as she fled the premises. If this got out that Isobella was the 'other' woman, then she would be exposed to the world. As soon as she got in the door she picked up the phone to ring James. "James, Isobella is going to be the talk of the town if this gets out. What can we do to protect her?" James was taken aback. "What do you mean, Mother?"

"The gossip has broken out about the city mayor having an affair; how can we stop this?" sobbed an upset Matilda. James was not at all sympathetic. "She created this drama, let her get out of it herself."

"You are heartless, James; Isobella is your sister," said a disappointed Matilda. But as always James was meant to make it all go away. But this was one time when he didn't want it to disappear, he wanted her to be exposed, let other people see who she really was.

Now it was time for James and Lillian to tell their children about their Aunty Isobella's affair before they heard it from other sources. They thought this was the best ever bit of news, at last their aunty was going to be exposed to the world. The eldest son Brad's reaction was straight from the horse's mouth. "I knew she was out to impress at Grandie's funeral, fancy snaring the city mayor, silly bugger." Isobella would not have been impressed with her nephew's remarks; mind you she probably forgot she even had a nephew.

But James had things closer to home to worry about. He had not been well for some time, and upon a visit to his doctor he was diagnosed with an illness that was going to rob him of a long life. Once all the tests were done he was told to enjoy what life he had left and to steer clear of stress, as his timeline was two years. This came as a terrible shock to his family, and himself.

It took a few weeks before James could bring himself to tell his mother, and this was at Lillian's insistence. Matilda had a right to know. James went to visit his mother to tell her about his health, and just as he had finished, the phone went. It was Isobella. "Mother, I don't know what to do, my boyfriend has found out about my affair, I'm frightened what he might do, not to me but to my lover." Matilda was in a panic. "Oh James, I'm really sad for you." Then all was brushed aside. What was going to happen to Isobella's lover, was the immediate worry. Wasn't that what always happened? Isobella had once again overshadowed James. This was when he missed Jessica.

But true to her worry, the following night the toy boy lay in wait for the new lover, and when he appeared at Matilda's, he attacked him. Matilda in desperation rang James to see if he would come and sort it out. This time he let fly with his emotions. "I am finished with Isobella's problems; don't bother to ring me again to sort things out for her. She is a selfless, shallow person, she can't even be civil to my family." James felt good to get this off his shoulders; whether Matilda listened was another matter.

Matilda had backed Isobella's new relationship all the way, as she could see advantages for her daughter. This is what she deserved, life owed her. The new lover had even taken Matilda to his flash home in the city while his wife was away on a cruise, and given her a grand tour. The house was fabulous, and the sea views were breathtaking. One could see the waves breaking as they reached the beach. This could all be Isobella's. But one thing had caught Matilda's eye, and that was the fabulous wine cellar, which was fully stocked. This was Matilda's dream come true. Here was a secure life for her daughter, and a wine cellar for herself, the bells were ringing loudly. At last Isobella would have a standing in life, one she deserved.

Of course, Matilda couldn't wait to tell James and Lillian about the city mayor's fabulous home with a fully stocked wine cellar. This immediately brought tears of laughter, as they could both see Matilda lost in the cellar among the bottles of wine. But for the city mayor, all they could see was a messed-up life, one he would live to regret, but this was for him to find out.

What of the toy boy? He was asked to leave, his time had expired. For goodness' sake, he was some years younger than Isobella; she was a cougar. In reality, a man with any knowledge of her past would steer well clear of this femme fatale spider.

The romance was blossoming and generous gifts were bestowed upon Isobella. Matilda's home was the meeting place for the lovers. They would sneak away for secret weekends together, all helped along by Matilda. This was going to be a fairy-tale ending for her darling Isobella. So many promises had been made by the lover, what was not to like about this romantic happening?

In the meantime, James's health was not getting any better, and suddenly his mother started to show some concern. Even Isobella came on board which surprised everyone, but deep down James was suspicious, there had to be something sinister ahead.

Lillian started to receive phone calls from Isobella. The first thing she wanted to know was if James was around, then she would ask, "Lillian, tell me the truth, is James getting better?" Lillian would tell the truth, and naively thought Isobella was genuine in her concern for her brother.

The love affair was still going strong, but sadly Matilda's health was also failing. She had been diagnosed with an incurable disease. Isobella was constantly with her mother, organising her life, and although Matilda loved her daughter, she had put up with her tantrums all her life.

James and Lillian saw a bit more of Isobella, as now they visited Matilda regularly.

Lillian was asked by Matilda if she would look after her vegetable garden, as she couldn't do much bending now. Every other day Lillian would busy herself in the garden, and when Isobella visited, she would barely acknowledge her, but then she was above Lillian who was just plain ordinary. One thing for sure, Isobella would not know what it was like to physically touch the earth beneath her, as she was far better than that. She couldn't get her beautiful nails soiled.

Matilda's 85th birthday was nearing, so James decided to put on a family party for her. No one was to cook; all the food would be brought in, at James's expense, so everyone could enjoy themselves. Isobella asked if she could invite a couple who were her friends, and who had visited Matilda with her on several occasions. Lillian also knew this couple as she had been to their home and purchased cleaning products.

The birthday went well, Matilda played her electric organ and everyone sang along, and she even had a couple of dances with the friend's husband. He was handsome, of tall stature and had a head of lovely silver hair and certainly knew how to move. James had to keep his eye on Matilda and her alcohol intake, in case her nastiness started to show, then it would all be over. Lillian could not see the connection for a friendship between Isobella and this couple, until she watched her dancing in the arms of this man, then it all became very clear. James put a phone call through to London so they could all talk to Jessica, especially Matilda, as she hadn't seen her daughter since she left for London. Jessica was a very independent and self-supporting young lady.

Matilda's health was failing so James and Lillian spent a lot more time at her home. One day while visiting Matilda, Isobella out of the blue came out with this statement as Matilda left the room. "Someone will be in for a big shock one day." James and Lillian looked at each other wondering why this remark was made. They just passed it off as some of Isobella's spiteful behaviour. But they did notice lately her behaviour was more hostile than usual towards them. Why was she like this? they wondered.

Sad times lay ahead, as James'a time frame of two years was nearing. Isobella was spasmodically in touch with Lillian inquiring about James's health. It was going to be sad for Matilda if James passed away before her, as was predicted to happen.

Then the bombshell! Isobella's romance was over. Her lover had been given the ultimatum by his wife. He was prepared to leave her for Isobella but the commitment was too binding for her, so she called it off. He wanted Isobella to sell her home and move to the city with him, but this meant the end of her independence. She didn't want to be a slave in the kitchen and have to wash his dirty clothes, that was for ordinary people. Isobella was better than ordinary. Such a devious soul.

Suddenly, gone were Matilda's dreams for her daughter's future. What would become of Isobella now? Why couldn't she settle for this prominent businessman and all the luxuries that went with him? But just as importantly, gone was Matilda's dream of being lost in the fully stocked wine cellar.

It didn't take long before the toy boy was back on the scene. Isobella needed an extra source of income, as she was only able to manage her mortgage and groceries on her waitress's wage, but it couldn't stretch any further. Anyhow he would do in the meantime.

The family received a call from London from Jessica to say she had met a lovely man and they were now married. It was a quiet affair and they were both happy.

# 4

# Matilda's Last Days

Matilda was now in hospital. She rang James one day. "I'm being taken to St Georges Hospital by ambulance for tests tomorrow, could you and Lillian drive up and meet me? Isobella can't take time off work."

The next day James and Lillian drove the four hours to St Georges to meet up with Matilda. There she was in the waiting room in her dressing gown, sitting in a wheelchair waiting to see the specialist. Lillian decided to leave the two of them together in case they wanted to have a private talk.

When she returned later and met up with James he looked like he had seen a ghost; the colour had gone from his cheeks and his eyes were very dark. He looked ill. "Are you okay, James, what is wrong?" asked a startled Lillian. James's voice was faint. "Mother is dying and they want her to stay here in hospital but she has demanded to be taken home." "Oh James, I'm so sorry," whispered Lillian.

"But that's not all. Mother told me she had left my share of her estate to Isobella, as she thought I was going to die before her, but now she is going first, she wants to change her will and leave it equally to the three of us, that's why she wants to go home. I told her not to worry, just to leave it as is, and stay and have the treatment that the doctor requested her to have.

"I would contest the will, and we would be entitled to three equal shares. Mother insisted that I couldn't do that, Isobella would have to go to court, she didn't want her in a court, it would be belittling for her. She wants to go home and see her solicitor, to put her mind at rest."

"Oh James, what a mess," sobbed Lillian.

"All my life I have played second fiddle to Isobella, but not any more. I have just worked out why all the interest in my health — she was hoping I would die first so she could get her hands on my share of the estate. For this she will pay. Remember when Isobella passed that comment 'Someone will be in for a big shock one day'? She was gloating, as she knew I had been left out of Mother's will. Thank goodness Jessica is away from all this," said an upset James. He added, "My parents expected me to spend every night and weekends building their home with no payment, over my dead body will Isobella reap the benefit from the fruits of my labour." Lillian was in total shock. How could Isobella be so devious and hateful towards another person, especially one of her own siblings?

"I have to go as Mother wants to talk to me before she leaves; will you come with me, Lillian?" asked James.

"No, I'm sorry but I don't want to become involved, this is a family affair, I know what Isobella is like, there will be repercussions, and I don't want to be implicated in any way," Lillian replied.

Off James went to try and convince his mother to stay at St Georges on the doctor's advice. But Matilda had to get back and do what had to be done, to spare her daughter the embarrassment of standing in a courtroom.

Matilda was taken back from St Georges in the ambulance to the local seaside hospital. After a couple of days she was released as there was nothing more that could be done for her. She asked James to come around the next morning, and when he arrived Matilda was not there. He waited until she arrived back. She had asked her home-help lady to drive her to her solicitor's where she changed her will and had her act as a witness. "James, I have changed my will, you, Jessica and Isobella get a third of everything. I couldn't go to my grave knowing I had left you out seeing I am leaving first, but promise me one thing: do not tell your sister, she must never know until I have passed away." This left James stunned; why did his mother not want his sister to know? Would this be because she would make everyone's life impossible? There had been many incidents of Isobella's tantrums over the years if life didn't pan out to her advantage.

The following week Matilda was admitted back to hospital as she was gravely ill. She was not a good patient, always complaining about the hospital food, which she let the staff know was not up to her standard. One evening while James and Lillian were visiting Matilda, her food was delivered. "Have a look at this, I am expected to eat this," she said and put the lid back on the food tray.

"Mother, you are in hospital, not a hotel, please try and be pleasant to these people, they are only trying to help you," said an upset James. "I will not eat this food," replied a hostile Matilda.

She kept to her word, and refused to eat all hospital food from that day forth. A couple of days later James received a call from the registrar of the hospital. "James, I'm sorry to have to ask you to do this, please try and get your mother to eat; she has not eaten for nearly a week and is causing concern in the ward. It is also affecting the patients around her." James was so angry he arranged for Isobella to meet him at the hospital when the night meal was due. When he arrived, there was Isobella sitting on the bed eating Matilda's dinner.

"What are you doing, that is Mother's food?" queried James. "She is not going to eat it, so I may as well eat it," said Isobella. James was beside himself, but he could see nothing he had to say was going to change the situation.

The following day when James went to visit his mother he was called into the office and told this: "James, you will have to arrange for your mother to go into a home, she cannot stay here in the hospital, as she is upsetting other patients." Poor James, this was so humiliating for him; not only was his mother refusing to eat, she was causing other patients distress. Now he had to try to get Matilda into a home. Was she going to behave herself somewhere else? This was a big worry for James as Isobella had voiced her opinion, and wanted Matilda to stay at the hospital, as it was very convenient for her to visit.

When James told Matilda she was leaving the hospital and going into a home, she performed. "I will not be going anywhere, I am staying here." This was exactly how James expected his mother to react. Suffice to say, that night Matilda took a turn for the worse and the next morning the family were called. Everyone gathered around

Matilda's bed where they spent the day, but there was very little conversation between James and Isobella. About 8.30pm Isobella decided to up and leave without a word to anyone. She walked out of the hospital with her head in the air. Matilda's breathing was getting faint, and at 10.00pm the nurse came in and said it wouldn't be long before Matilda would pass away.

Where had Isobella gone, how was James to get in touch with her to let her know that Matilda only had a short time left on this earth? He rang her cellphone, no answer, he rang her home phone, no answer, so he left a message on her cellphone to tell her to come to the hospital as soon as possible. At 10.30 Matilda peacefully passed away without her darling Isobella at her bedside. It was her granddaughter, Amelia, who held her hand till the end.

James left another message on Isobella's cellphone to say their mother had passed away. Then all hell broke loose. Down the hospital corridor came a clatter of high heels, and a voice yelling, "Why wasn't I told she was dying? She was my mother, I should have been with her."

"Aunty Isobella, she was my father and Aunty Jessica's mother too. Dad tried to contact you, don't come in here causing a scene," sobbed Amelia, who hated her aunty for the way she treated her father.

Amelia's mind went back many years, to the day when she was staying with her grandmother. Isobella had come charging into the bedroom where Matilda was sitting on her bed, and as Matilda stood up Isobella tried to push her over in a rage. Amelia jumped out of bed to try to protect her grandmother. "Leave my grandmother alone," she told Isobella. "You keep out of my way in future, you little bitch," warned Isobella as she stomped out of the room. Amelia had never forgiven her for this.

No wonder her friendships were so fleeting; she had no love or compassion to share with anyone, it all went on herself, in other words no one else mattered. Now her 'society of beautiful people' had lost another member. Was she the only one left?

The day of Matilda's funeral had finally arrived.

Following the hearse into the churchyard was a vehicle carrying the lonely figure of Isobella. James and his family were in the second car, as he had not been invited to travel with his sister; this was reserved for Isobella only. This was *her* mother's funeral. The service and burial went without a hitch. James was sad that Jessica couldn't make it out to their mother's funeral, as mother and daughter had not seen each other for many years, since she had left for London. But neither had James seen Jessica and he really missed her. Afterwards everyone gathered at the church hall for afternoon tea.

Lillian looked around and noticed Isobella sitting at a table with her friends. She recognised the out-of-town couple who were at Matilda's 85th birthday and the toy boy, but the others she had never seen before. One lady in particular took her eye: she was a buxom blonde, and talked with a loud Australian accent. This seemed out of character for Isobella to have a friend that could have been her rival. Lillian wondered how and where these two had met. This friendship was a complete mystery!

Many relatives had come to say their goodbyes to Matilda mainly because she had been Bartholomew's wife. Everyone knew how fickle she was; some were able to overlook this, others weren't so forgiving, but felt it was their duty to be there. Isobella made no attempt to speak with any relatives; she did the same at her father's funeral, nothing had changed. She sat with her friends and talked about everyone, acting as the superior being that she thought she was. Lots of remarks were made about Isobella by relatives, as they had experienced this spoilt behaviour at Bartholomew's funeral.

A week had just passed since Matilda's funeral when James received a phone call from London. It was Jessica's husband to say that she had been in an accident and lay seriously ill in hospital. She had requested to see James, so could he please come over and be with her. This was a shock and he was heartbroken — Jessica was his favourite sister. They had both suffered in their younger years from Isobella's tantrums.

James contacted Isobella to let her know about Jessica. He didn't ask her to accompany him to London as she had not been asked for. Isobella showed very little emotion towards her sister's plight, but at least she had been informed.

The flight to London seemed to take forever for James and Lillian. On arrival at the hospital they were greeted by their brother-in-law whom they had never met. He took them to Jessica's bedside, only to find her asleep. He bent down and gently woke her, and when she stirred there was James. The tears started as they held each other's hand. The bed was surrounded by machines all of which Jessica was hooked up to. They stayed with her until she drifted off to sleep. Sadly that night she passed away, but she had seen her beloved James. They stayed in London for her funeral, as she wanted to be buried in their home town of Salisbury.

# 5

# The Battle Begins

On returning home from London, James went around to his mother's home only to be greeted by Isobella. "You can't come in, this is my home now because mother left it to me. She left me your share of her estate and now that Jessica's gone I get it all, you get nothing. I was with her when she made her will so I know how she left things. I told her that you were going to die first and not to leave our family money to your wife and kids." Instead of being shocked, James was amused, as he knew something that Isobella didn't. This was one last promise he had made to his mother that he was able to keep. This meant so much to him, because in the past his promises had been broken through no fault of his own but because of Isobella's interference. Now who was going to be in for 'a big shock'?

Matilda's solicitor rang James and asked him to come

down to his office. "I have been trying to get in touch with Isobella but I can't reach her at her home," he said. "You won't catch her at her home because she has moved into mother's home," replied James "Why has she done that?" he asked. "She said that mother left her the home in her will," said James.

"That is not true, your mother left her estate a third to each of her three children," the solicitor reported. James already knew this but had not let on to anyone except Lillian, so acted surprised. The solicitor then went on to say, "Now that Jessica has passed away and there are no children, the estate will go to you and Isobella. You are both trustees to your mother's will." James knew this was not going to be easy, in fact it was going to be impossible. Once Isobella found out the truth about the will she was going to be one insane lady. "You can contact her and tell her about the will, I don't want to be around when she is told," said James. How would Isobella react when she found out she was not the sole 'heiress' that suddenly she thought she was because of Jessica's death? This made James feel really good right deep down in his heart, as for the first time in his life he knew something his sister didn't.

Three weeks had gone by since Matilda passed away, and still the solicitor could make no contact with Isobella. He had left messages on her phone and written to her but still received no replies. He had to explain the contents of the will to her. He rung James and said, "We will give her another week and if she doesn't make contact with me we will have to take action."

A week went by and still no news from Isobella, so now was time to act. Matilda's solicitor asked James to meet him at the family home at a given time. Together they put a padlock on the gate so Isobella could not get onto the property; hopefully this would get her attention.

This was all that was needed. An irate Isobella rocked up at the solicitor's office accusing James of locking her out of her property. Now the home truths had to be revealed by the solicitor. "Isobella, I have been trying to contact you for days but you have not answered my calls or letters. Please sit down as I read your mother's will." "I know what was in her will, she told me what she had done," interrupted Isobella. "I'm sorry but your mother made an updated will and things have changed," he said. "What do you mean?!" shouted Isobella.

As he proceeded to read out the will, Isobella's face turned to stone. "No, this is not true, I helped mother word her will, I know James gets nothing and now that Jessica's gone it is all mine!" she ranted. "I'm sorry but this is her last will and testament, so this has to be obeyed. You cannot go back into the home as it is not yours. You and James are both trustees to the will. I know this is what your mother wanted, as I asked her about changing her will, and she insisted this was what she wanted," replied the solicitor. "I know it is that bloody James, he has forced mother into changing her will, I will get him for this!" screamed Isobella. "I will contest the will and take him to court," and off she stormed slamming the door. So much for Matilda trying to keep her darling daughter from appearing in court.

Why had Matilda asked James not to say anything to Isobella about her changing the will, this he could not understand!

This was just the show of arrogance that confirmed to the solicitor that James had an up-and-coming battle on his hands.

The next appearance from Isobella was at the solicitor's office to let him know she was going to contest the will. She was going to go for all the estate, James was going to get nothing. "If you contest the will you can no longer be a trustee, you have to relinquish this position, therefore have no further say in what happens to the estate," she was told by Matilda's solicitor. "This cannot be right, I will get another opinion," snapped Isobella as she stomped out.

It didn't take long for her to find out that the facts she had been given were indeed true. "I've come to let you know I have hired a lawyer and we are going to take James to the cleaners; this wasn't left to him, my father didn't love James like he loved me and Jessica," Isobella announced. "Now it will all be mine." "I will get you to sign this form releasing you from trustee duties," stated Matilda's solicitor. Isobella was not at all happy about this, but she had weighed up what was more important, and the inheritance won out.

Matilda's solicitor contacted James to let him know he was now sole trustee. He could not believe his sister would give up her trustee position, and have no say in the distributing of the estate.

Isobella had not been allowed back into the family home since the locks were changed. On entering the home James noticed the beautiful old piano that his mother had promised to his daughter Amelia had been removed and was no longer there. When questioned by the solicitor, Isobella denied she knew anything about the missing piano.

When the time was right, James contacted Matilda's solicitor to let him know he was putting the home on the market. He listed it with a real estate agent that he knew. The next morning, they both met to put up the 'For Sale' signs. After a couple of days, James received a call to say they had been removed. He went down and put up new ones, but they also mysteriously disappeared. No one knew who was interfering with the signs, but it was obvious that someone didn't want the home to be sold.

One day the real estate agent rang James to tell him she had a strange experience. "An out-of-town couple came for a viewing, and they brought their camera, and took photos in each room. It is not usual for clients to do this, I am a little worried." "Who were these people, did they give you a name?" asked James. When the agent said who they were, James knew immediately it was the older couple, friends of Isobella's who had been at Matilda's 85th birthday.

Isobella had sent them to take photos of each room so she could see if anything had been removed. James was one step ahead of his sister knowing her devious ways, so he had left everything as he found it. Not that it really mattered, as she had no say in any future estate matters. She had made her choice.

Six months had now passed and finally the family home was sold. There had been no verbal contact between James and Isobella since Matilda's passing, although her lawyer had sent a request to Matilda's solicitor asking for items from the family home to be passed on to his client. This James agreed to, and arranged for them to be dropped off at his mother's solicitor.

One day while James and Lillian were out in their garden a car drove up their driveway, and out stepped a gentleman with a bunch of papers that had to signed for. James asked, "What are these, who are they from?" "I have been asked to deliver them, they are court documents, that is why I have to get you to sign for them, so the court knows you have received them," replied the gentleman.

James and Lillian sat down to see what had been delivered. They were called 'affidavits'. Each one had been written by different people; there were in fact five of them. Not having had anything to do with courts before, neither James nor Lillian knew what they were. That was until they opened them and started to read the absolute rubbish and lies written in these papers.

James headed straight down to Matilda's solicitor and confronted him with them. "What the hell are these all about? They are full of lies. What do we do with them? I want nothing to do with these people, in fact I will ignore them." "I'm sorry, James, but you can't do that, they have to be replied to. These people have sworn on oath that this is what happened, so in their eyes everything they have written is deemed true, unless proven otherwise. You will have to hire a lawyer and reply to these affidavits," said the solicitor. "But this will cost a lot of money; it's not my doing that Isobella is contesting the will, why do I have to pay for a lawyer?" replied an irate James. "That is the law, James, there is nothing else we can do. I will get you a good lawyer if you want me to." James agreed to this, as he didn't really know any lawyers that handled court work.

Now James had to deal with the household contents seeing the house was sold. He asked a second-hand dealer to give a price for the house lot. Lillian kept a few pieces of crystal and a couple of ornaments that she liked. The dealer came to take everything away, and decided rather than pack all the ornaments, etc. away, he would leave them in the cabinet and carefully barrow them out to the waiting truck. Sadly, with the weight of the crockery and ornaments, the back came off the cabinet and everything inside fell and broke on the concrete. This was hard to take, to see a lifetime of personal items lying on the ground in pieces. Just as well Matilda didn't witness this, it would have broken her heart, as would have a lot of other goings-on.

Now James and Lillian had time to sit down and fully read the affidavits, as they had previously just glanced quickly through them.

Isobella stated in hers 'that James had coerced his mother into changing her will in his favour. She knew there was another will that Matilda had made, because she was with her the day she went to her solicitors, and they had discussed what was going to be written in the will, and James was not in it, because he was going to die. Matilda wanted to leave her estate to Isobella and Jessica, that was until James exerted undue influence on his mother. She was frightened of James, he was a bully, so he must have threatened mother.' Upon reading this, James was stunned that so many lies could be written under oath, but then this was his sister Isobella; things had never changed and even as she grew older she never outgrew the thought that life owed her. Her attitude had remained the same. This was certainly proven as James went on to read the other affidavits.

He didn't need this, he had enough issues of his own to worry about. Was this the opportunity Isobella was waiting for, to break him before the estate was distributed?

Two other affidavits were written in a similar pattern all stating that they had on very few occasions seen James and Lillian at Matilda's home. That Matilda had told them that she was leaving the home to Isobella as she had cared for her mother, and James was financially well enough off, so didn't need the money. Also, that James was a bully.

These were the exact words that Isobella had said about her brother in her affidavit.

But it was the fourth one written by the out-of-town couple, Isobella's friends, the ones that Lillian had brought cleaning products from, that was the final nail in the coffin. The contents of this affidavit were untrue and outrageous, and to think it had been written under oath was even more unthinkable. It was directed at Lillian, the innocent party in all this. After reading it she ran up to her bedroom and lay on the bed sobbing her heart out; how could anyone write something so cruel? When James read it he was horrified, but this was all Isobella's doing, it was her wicked mind working overtime. She was out for revenge, but why Lillian?

The affidavit read: 'On a named date while visiting Matilda in hospital, as I entered the ward I couldn't see her in her bed, all I could see was her daughter-in-law lying on the bed, and when I came closer there was Matilda, squashed under Lillian. I couldn't hear her breathing so I told Lillian three times to get off Matilda, but she took no notice, so I had to pull her off.'

These were blatant lies, it had never happened. If she was worried about Matilda, why didn't she ring for a nurse? Lillian knew these people, why would they say this? When she recovered from the shock, she was so angry, as she thought this was bordering on slander, so drove down to the local police station. She spoke with the police super-intendent and let him read what was written. This is what he said: "I'm sorry, even if it is not true it has been writ-ten under oath, so is deemed as the truth by this person, so now you have to prove otherwise." "But it's not true, it's lies, I couldn't do that to my mother-in-law, I respected her," sobbed Lillian. "Sadly, this is the course of justice, we cannot do anything," he replied sympathetically.

Where to from here? The next step was to take it to the newly appointed lawyer. He would be able to offer advice as to what had to happen. "You will have to speak to the hospital registrar, and because there has been a date mentioned when this incident happened, it will make it easier for him to check the records," he said.

Upon meeting the registrar of the hospital, he told James and Lillian there was a lot of work involved. He would have to go back through the hospital records, and speak to staff that were on duty on that particular day, as now one year had passed since Matilda had passed away. This was going to take some time, but he promised to contact James when he had it all sorted out, and would supply a written statement.

A few weeks later another affidavit was delivered. This one was written by a friend of Isobella's who was employed as the restaurant manageress where Isobella worked as a waitress. She had written a very impressive curriculum vitae, stating she was employed as a secretary to a top Australian government official before coming to New Zealand. Lillian realised this must be the buxom blonde that was sitting at Isobella's table at Matilda's funeral. Like the rest of the affidavits she had lied and stated that she had never seen James or Lillian at Matilda's house. This was another victim that had been caught in Isobella's web.

After all the affidavits had been responded to, the lawyers from both sides presented their cases. If this could be sorted amicably by both parties, then it wouldn't have to go to court. A hearing was organised between the two lawyers at a settlement conference presided over by a judge. Isobella would settle her claim for an extra $45,000 more than James, but in a counteroffer James agreed to give her $20,000. Anything above this amount could not be justified by James, as he wanted his mother's will to stay as it was intended.

The counteroffer was not good enough for Isobella, and as it was on James's terms, not hers, she instructed her lawyer to take it all the way to the Family Court. Now they had to apply for a date with the Family Court. It would take at least another year before a date would be allocated, with priority given to more urgent custody and access cases.

In the meantime, James's lawyer received a letter from Isobella's lawyer saying they were not pursuing several of the claims that had been laid against James. This was helpful for James as it narrowed the issues in dispute, and meant that the evidence from the couple that had targeted Lillian had now been thrown out. The opposing lawyer must have realised how ridiculous this affidavit was and that the accusations were not true. By now he would have received a report from the hospital registrar clearing Lillian of any misdeeds regarding Matilda.

# 6

# The Family Court Hearing

A date and time was now set at the Family Court, and two days had been allocated for the hearing. It was now three years since Matilda had passed away, and still not a verbal word had been exchanged between James and Isobella.

The day of the hearing had arrived. Isobella, looking the fashion plate that she was, and her web of friends had taken over the waiting room. Because James wanted to keep this family matter strictly within the family, he had not brought in any outside parties, so there was just himself, Lillian and their two children. They stood in the hallway, not wanting to be in the same room as Isobella and her tangled web of supporters.

In the courtroom sat the judge at the bench. All people giving evidence and supporters were allowed into the courtroom. Questions were fired at James by Isobella's lawyer who had obtained information on all assets owned by James and his family trust. But somewhere amid all his research he had James's information mixed up with his son Brad's assets. This caused some confusion. Then he went on to ask James about his interest in his mother, because as far as he could ascertain by all the affidavits filed, he was not a frequent visitor at her place. "My sister is nothing short of a liar, I can't believe the lies that have been told. I visited my mother often and so did Lillian, but we only saw the couple there, plus the toy boy but none of the others, as we don't even know them," said an irate James. "Perhaps that is why you don't know them, you never visited often," fired back the lawyer. With this James lost it: "I am not wasting my breath on my sister, you can believe what you like!" The judge intervened and told James to stick to answering the questions. "Why did you coerce your mother into changing her will? You are affluent, you don't need the money. Isobella is more in need than you, that is why the estate was left to her in the first will." The judge reminded the lawyer that the 'undue influence claim' had been withdrawn. James was ropable, this sure was one mongrel lawyer that Isobella had employed to defend her. But then it was understandable, as she was no better herself. After a hard grilling, James was asked to stand down and now it was Isobella's turn on the stand to be cross-examined. Unfortunately, James's lawyer was not the aggressive type; he was going to take a soft but firm approach, and let the judge know that James had helped his sister financially when she needed it. "Isobella, I believe when you needed financial help, James was there for you." "No, that is not true, I can't recall him ever helping me," she said. "His wife authorised for you to pick up money from their bank when you needed it."

"No, I don't think that is right. In fact no, I never asked Lillian for any money," lied Isobella. With that, James's lawyer questioned her further. "You own your own home, how did you get your loan?" "My father arranged it for me at his bank before he died," she lied again. "That is not true, James secured it for you through his bank, is that not right?" he questioned. "No, I remember my father doing it for me, not James," replied Isobella. This was going nowhere; it didn't matter what James's lawyer said, Isobella was determined to undermine her brother. This was when James wished he had employed a mongrel lawyer, one who would have torn Isobella to shreds. He also wished he had asked his bank manager to verify that he was telling the truth. Now it was time for her to stand down and make her way back to her lawyer, who was all grins as she returned.

The next person called to the bench was the blonde Australian lady, the one with the impressive work resumé. The judge asked her how she was involved. "I am a friend of Isobella's and often went to visit her mother, but I never saw her brother or his wife at her home. In fact, I never knew she had a brother until he was pointed out to me at Matilda's funeral," she replied. James's lawyer asked her the question again: "Can you be sure you didn't see James or his wife at Matilda's home? Surely you must have seen them, if only on one occasion?" "No, never; as I said, I didn't even know she had a brother," replied the Australian lady in a commanding voice. The judge was busy writing things down, and she seemed to be taken by this lady.

After the first day finished, the judge asked both James and Isobella to attend court the next morning. On the second day she spoke with them separately in her summing up, and said she would notify them when she had made her decision.

Another year had passed and still there was no decision from the judge. James and Lillian, like everyone else except Isobella, thought a will that was now left 50/50 was binding, that there could be no counterclaims, as this was fair for both parties, but first and foremost this was Matilda's last will and testament. How did anyone including a family member have the right to contest this? James and Lillian were convinced that the will would remain as it was intended, there was no doubt in their minds.

A will was a binding document. But this did not prove to be true; a judge had the power to overturn a will if indeed they saw fit to do so, even if it was totally against the wishes of the deceased person. James and Lillian had never heard of this before, but did not think for one minute that this would happen in their case, as one was not favoured over the other.

Isobella had made the family business public by telling people that her brother had contested her mother's will. She had a twisted mind, so everyone else was always to blame. This was to make James look like the bad guy, and for her to be portrayed as the innocent party, so all the attention would be focused on her. Even when James and his daughter flew overseas to an aunty's 90th birthday, people were there from James's home town, and they approached him about his underhandedness regarding his mother's will. There was no escape, the poison had spread.

One day by chance James ran into his ex-bank manager, and a conversation between the two turned back to the day when he had come into the bank to arrange a loan for his sister. He wanted to know how it all worked out, and was his sister still in her home. When James mentioned what he had just gone through with Isobella, he was horrified: "Why didn't you call me as a witness? I would have told the truth about the house loan," he said. "We didn't want it to go outside the family," replied James. "Why be so gracious, James, it hasn't done you any favours," was his reply. "As a family we have suffered so much pain; I don't class Isobella as my sister any more, to me she is a stranger," said a sad James, as his mind went back to Jessica.

Months went by, and so did Christmas, and still no decision from the judge. Then one day a letter arrived from James's lawyer stating, 'Your sister's lawyer has asked that she get an advance from the estate funds as she is in need of money.'

Due to the pain she had inflicted on James, did she honestly think he would make it easy for her? This was not going to be a happening thing. He contacted his lawyer and told him, "Under no circumstances will Isobella be paid any money until the judge has made her decision." If Isobella hadn't been so greedy and accepted James's counteroffer of $20,000, then she would have had her money years ago, but this was her decision, and a bad one at that. Both lawyers' fees were steadily mounting and would continue to do so until the estate was settled.

Isobella's lawyer was annoyed that James would not release some money, but as the sole trustee, this was his call. He probably needed money for his services to the estate, but James was going to be just as brutal to him as he was to James in court. Now it was his turn to call the shots; they may have won the battle in the court, but this was payback.

Finally in March, James and Isobella both received a written copy of the 'Decision of the Judge'. This paper laid out all her findings, and how she reached her final verdict. At last this was going to be laid to rest, and a normal life could be resumed by all.

As James read through the judge's report and recommendations, the outcome was not as he expected. Although the judge had found that Isobella and her acquaintances had made substantial criticism of James, which was unfounded as it was not meant to be a persecution of character but it had turned out that way, she only found one of Isobella's friends creditable and that was the Australian lady. She found that 'her evidence at times had a somewhat colourful style' and that she was endeavouring to tell the truth, so she accepted her evidence.

James and Lillian were shocked to read this, as they had never seen this woman at Matilda's home, ever. If she had visited the home she would have seen a portrait of Isobella aged five years, James aged thirteen years, and Jessica aged three, hanging on the lounge wall. In her affidavit, she said she didn't know that Isobella had a brother until he was pointed out to her at Matilda's funeral. How could a judge get it so wrong? Had she been blinded by the Australian lady's previous work record, or her overwhelming presence?

In her summing up, the judge overruled Matilda's will and awarded Isobella a substantial sum, well above what James was to receive. The 50/50 will was revoked. James was upset by this ruling, not from the money aspect but because his mother's last wishes had been overturned, but as always, everything worked in Isobella's favour.

Now that the decision had been made by the judge against Matilda's will, rendering it invalid, it was time to distribute the estate.

The lawyers from both sides were desperately in need

of their money, as this had been going on for four years. The huge lawyers' bills that were amassed by James and Isobella were to be the first payments from the estate, thus eroding half of the estate that the parents had spent a lifetime building. They both would have been angry that this amount of money had gone to lawyers.

This was all brought about by Isobella contesting the will in the first place. In the end, it was the lawyers who benefited most from Bartholomew and Matilda's estate, as it was quite a nest egg they had built up. Isobella was very smug having been awarded more money than James, not taking into account how much money was lost in lawyers' fees. She was not up there with finances; as long as she had money to spend, then that was the crux of her world. To get one over James was worth losing thousands of dollars for.

After the court ruling was over and the estate was paid out, Isobella's lawyer sent a letter stating that she wanted the family portrait that hung on the lounge wall in the family home. James had put the portrait away as he did not want Isobella's photo anywhere in his house. He agreed that she could have it.

Lillian was furious; she did not want James's photo hanging in Isobella's home so he could be ridiculed in front of her friends. She did the unthinkable. Unbeknown to James she hid the photo where it could not be found, then explained that she had no idea where it had gone. This was Lillian's way of dealing with her self-centred sister-in-law. Besides, as she had no feelings for James, why would she want a reminder of him in her home, other than to say bad things about him? This was not going to be happening thing.

Isobella might have been the glamour puss on the outside, but inside she had the heart of a twisted willow. Revenge was always on her mind; why, one would never know, as she always got what she wanted in life. The ones that were closest to her suffered most. Matilda was frustrated with her daughter, James and Jessica disliked her, Lillian felt very little for her, and her niece and nephew just could not be bothered with her.

This would not worry or deter Isobella; she still had herself to love, that was all she was interested in. Life for her was different now, as she had money. As was predicted, the toy boy was tossed out again, she didn't need him any more, she could support herself. First she bought herself a nice car, as she wanted to look important, she deserved that privilege at least.

It was now five years since Matilda had passed away and still not a verbal word had passed between James and Isobella. Anything that James felt for his sister had long gone; to him she didn't exist, and he now classed himself as an only child, with no siblings. Lillian thought this was a bit harsh, but then she didn't have to live with Isobella for all the years that James and Jessica had. Especially when things didn't go her way. Perhaps she might have felt the same if she had been James.

One day Amelia rang Lillian to say she had been on the internet and seen Aunty Isobella's photo on a dating sight. "You should have seen it, Mum, she said she was forty-one but I know she is forty-nine. She was wearing sunglasses and looked very glam. She wants someone who is good looking, likes nice clothes and shoes, and has no baggage." Lillian replied, "It sounds like she wants a wardrobe, not a person," and they both had a laugh. "Pity help the next victim that gets caught in her web."

Now that Isobella had left James's life forever, he felt a

weight lifted off his shoulders, one which he had carried around for a long time. Lillian now fully understood what James had gone through and saw Isobella for what she was. But as one looked back, it was her parents that helped make her what she was. They were the ones that pushed James aside and afforded her everything she wished for. Jessica was always the child caught in the middle and she learnt to be resourceful, as she was not the beauty that her sister was.

James's health was starting to pick up again now that all the stress was behind him. He had surprised his doctors by living well past the time limit they had given him. A lot of this was to do with new cancer pills coming on stream; as one finished its usefulness, another new one appeared, many thanks to modern medicine.

Months had passed, nine in fact, when one day out of the blue James received a phone call from a lady with a prominent Australian accent: "You may not remember me, but I have rung to apologise for filing a false affidavit after your mother's death." James immediately clicked as to who this was — Isobella's friend, the buxom blonde. "I have inquired around town and have not heard a bad word said against you. The affidavit I filed was false, I was asked to sign it by Isobella. I am sorry for all the stress I have caused you. I just want to let you know that the piano that went missing from your mother's house was brought here to my garage by your sister. It has been in my garage ever since then. I wanted it removed and tried to contact Iso-bella but she never answered her phone, so I went to her home and found my ex-partner's car parked at the back of her house. I am truly sorry." James was in disbelief; this was the woman's affidavit that the judge believed to be true, and used in her summing up, in fact in her decision-making. Both James and Lillian knew she had lied right from the start.

Here was a woman scorned, one who had obviously fallen out with Isobella over a man, and who felt it her duty to tell the truth, although it was too late. But in all this, the truth was revealed. Imagine how James felt: here was a witness who had perjured herself while under oath, and may have in fact helped to sway the judge's decision in Isobella's favour. This left James feeling somewhat let down.

"I am angry to think Isobella may have won by foul means, but that is the nature of the beast," said James. "This lady should have been prosecuted for lying under oath," but for him it was all over. The past was best forgotten, no one wanted to go back there again.

# 7

# An Insight into Isobella

Each fortnight James would get a phone call from his overseas aunty to see how he was. On this particular day she had a message for James. "I had a call from Isobella asking me if I thought there would be any chance of a reconciliation with you." "And what did you say, Aunty?" inquired James. "I told her I didn't think that would ever be a happening thing." "You are so right, I never want any more lies told about me or my family," said James. "Isobella will never be any different, her nature will never change, and we know who to blame for that. If I wanted something, she would want the same. I can remember taking a girlfriend on a date and she performed because she wanted to come, so my parents told me I had to take her. Then she ran back to them with stories, things that never happened, only in her mind. Isobella was a good storyteller but not all her stories were truthful. Poor Jessica's life was also made unbearable at times and that is why she left home at a young age and went abroad."

Being the youngest was not easy for Jessica as she was often blamed for things that were not of her doing. She was not into make-up and fashion like her sister. The two girls were so different, they had very little in common. On the other hand, Isobella lived for her fashion; she would never buy her clothes locally, someone might have the same, which would be the worst dilemma. The local shops were not upmarket enough for her, so she would travel for miles searching for clothes that no one else had, or couldn't possibly afford. Isobella would not be seen twice in the same outfit; once it was worn it became a cast-off.

She was very young and headstrong when she first married. Her husband worked long hours, trying to bring home a healthy pay packet to keep the home fires burning. But this did not suffice; she wanted more, so this relationship was never going to work. This was one area in life that Isobella suffered; sadly she didn't share her love. If things didn't go her way, all those around her suffered. Many men were infatuated with her; she certainly had the looks and the body, and dressed to impress, and did exactly that: impressed the opposite sex. She was never short of suitors but then she was very picky; the better looking, the higher up the pecking order one became.

Isobella didn't have a lot of friends; she was a bit of a loner and a user. To look at her she seemed to have it all and at times she was even a little likeable but these moments were few and far between. This was the story of Isobella's life. Was it ever going to be any different?

# 8

# Has Isobella Met Her Match?

Isobella met her next victim online. He answered her posting. Here was this forty-three-year-old in her own mind, but in reality she was nearing fifty-two, a glamorous brunette who loved clothes and dancing, and wanted to meet someone with similar interests. There was to be no baggage, meaning no kids.

She had many replies, but none of them was the man of her dreams, until Mr C arrived on the scene. By reading his posting he had everything she was looking for, but first and foremost he was an extremely good-looking middle-aged man, and was financially secure. For Isobella, looks came before anything else, and now she had found the man she was searching for, the rest would follow.

They agreed to meet for a coffee at a little café where they could chat and find out about each other. On the given day Isobella arrived early and went inside to find a table for them. As soon as Mr C walked through the door, Isobella's heart skipped a beat; true to his listing he was a very handsome man. After greeting each other, they ordered their coffees and began chatting. Isobella lay her cards on the table, whether truthful or not, about herself.

"My partner passed away some time ago and I am on my own. I own my own home and am financially secure, my mother passed away and left me a small inheritance so I was able to buy a nice upmarket car." She did look the part, she was beautifully dressed, although her neckline was exceedingly low, but it was exposing what it was meant to. She knew the tricks of the trade, and how to lure unsuspecting prey into her tangled web.

Mr C, on the other hand, was a mature gentleman, with a tinge of silver in his hair and dressed in a beautifully cut sports jacket and designer jeans. He was a semi-retired businessman who had also lost his partner. He still had business interests which took him away a lot, and he was looking for someone compatible to share his life with, but was he?

If he was looking for someone sincere, Isobella was not the one for him, but if they were two of a kind, then life was about to get interesting. Mr C did not divulge his financial position. He looked out the window of the café and saw kids leaning over his car, so he excused himself and went outside. Isobella peeped out to see what was happening, and there parked outside the café was the most beautiful blood-red Lamborghini. Was this his car? He told the kids they could admire his car but not to touch it.

After re-entering the café, he sat down and they resumed talking.

"Is that beautiful car yours?" asked Isobella. "Yes, it is

my pride and joy. I love driving it on the open road, let me tell you, it can go fast," he said proudly. Isobella knew then that she was on to a good thing. A good-looking guy with a blood-red Lamborghini, what more could one ask for? If only Matilda was still around, she would be so proud of her daughter. But she wasn't thought about much any more, because she had double-crossed Isobella over her will.

Suddenly the sun was smiling once again on Isobella. It had been a while since the city mayor had disappeared off the scene, but now there was someone new and exciting, and rich to boot.

As they left the café they walked to Isobella's car together. Mr C leaned over and gave her a peck on her cheek, and thanked her for a lovely afternoon. "I will contact you in a couple of days, and perhaps we could meet again," he said. "I would like that very much," replied Isobella.

Several days had passed and she had not yet received that long-awaited phone call. Where was this mystery man, why hadn't he called? In desperation she went back on to her computer and, lo and behold, his post was still there on the dating scene. Why hadn't he removed it? He was seeing her now; this was not on. Isobella was seething; she wanted this man, and what Isobella wanted, she usually got. If she didn't hear from him, how could she contact him? She didn't have his phone number, in actual fact she knew very little about him, as he had not discussed his business or where he lived. All she knew was he drove a blood-red Lamborghini, of which she didn't get the number off the plate, otherwise she would have been able to track him down. Isobella's mind was working overtime; she was all out to get this man.

Just as she was about to give up, Isobella received the long-awaited phone call. She knew she had to stay calm and not upset him, otherwise he would dump her. "I'm sorry, Isobella, I was called out of the country unexpectedly on business, that is why I haven't contacted you, but I'm here now. Can we arrange to meet again?" All too eager she answered, "Oh yes, I would like that." With that, another date was made for the same café.

Isobella arrived early and sat in her car, as she wanted to see the blood-red Lamborghini arrive. Around the corner it came, drawing glances and wows from all directions. To think one day it could be her driving this car. Isobella's mind went into overdrive, she was so excited, but she deserved this, as Matilda had always told her she should have the best.

Out of the car climbed Mr C. He looked a million dollars in his royal blue velvet jacket and classy jeans. But then Isobella was not going to be outdone. She had spent the whole of yesterday searching for the perfect dress to wow her new man. She carried herself well and looked a picture. Her new Gucci sunglasses just finished off the expensive outfit, they added a touch of class. Isobella walked up to Mr C and greeted him: "You look very dashing, if I may say so." "You are some attractive lady yourself," he said to Isobella. This sent her into a spin. Was he going to be an easy catch? she asked herself.

As they walked to the café together they drew glances from all the passers-by: what an attractive couple. The waitresses at the coffee shop remembered them, and fell over each other wanting to serve them. They had wondered who they were when they called last time, and now they were back. They may have been Hollywood stars; rumours started all around the café as to who they were, and the blood-red Lamborghini parked outside the door, only the very rich owned a car like that.

As they were sipping their coffees, Mr C reached over and took Isobella's hand. "I haven't stopped thinking about you since our last meeting," he said. Isobella gave him a cheeky grin; she was frightened to speak in case she said the wrong thing. They chatted over their coffees, with Isobella talking nine to the dozen about herself. He was a good listener. Several hours had passed before they both emerged from the café. He thanked Isobella, and once again sealed their meeting with a kiss on her cheek, then walked her back to her Audi.

As Mr C walked back to his Lamborghini, Isobella suddenly realised she had done all the talking and still had no information on him. She waited in her car until he drove past, and quickly jotted down his registration number. Now she was no longer in the dark, she could hunt him down. If he wasn't going to give out information about himself, then she would make it her business to find out. This was how Isobella's mind worked. She would wait to see how long it took Mr C to contact her again, before she started her stalking.

To Isobella's surprise it only took a couple of days for the call to arrive. He invited her to his property for dinner on Saturday night, as he wanted to cook for her and show off his culinary skills. Oh my God, he can also cook, that was another stamp of approval. Mr C gave her his address and property number, and asked her to come around 5.30pm. Every day she found surprises about this man, which made her think he was definitely for her.

Isobella flew into a panic; what was she going to wear? She wanted to make a statement, she had to look seductive, this was her big chance to win over Mr C and his

Lamborghini. The next day she went on a shopping spree; the first port of call was the lingerie department. Isobella was in her element: such beautiful undergarments, what would colour would she settle for? Black might not be the right colour for a first date; perhaps a pretty pink to bring a little innocence to the bedroom setting, but then she spied the flame-red set; this would set any passion alight, and it would match the Lamborghini. This is what Isobella settled for, and along with matching red nail polish and lipstick, this would add an elegant touch, she told herself.

Now for the next layer. Forget a dress, she needed something that was sexy, and easy to slip off, so settled for a low-cut knitted top. Then came the trousers; should she buy something loose and free-flowing or something really fitting to show off her fab figure? Fab figure trousers were her final choice. She could just see herself on Mr C's plush suite with her legs dangling over the side, and her loose top slipping to show off her beautiful tanned shoulders. She would team this up with her very expensive crocodile-skin stilettos, which she would kick off as she walked across the plush carpet.

Matilda would be trying to take leave from her world above, to come back to earth and cheer on her darling daughter, although she was only remembered now and again when it suited Isobella.

Saturday had finally arrived. Several times Isobella had thought about cruising past the address she had been given, but decided to let it be a surprise on the special night. Anyhow she knew in her own mind what it was like, as this was a fairy-tale story, so everything would be of the best. She had never been to this side of the city and was surprised at the luxurious homes dotted along the streets. She found the street name, and now had to look for the letterbox with the given number. As she drove to the end, there before her, down a driveway lined with huge elm trees, set on an acreage stood a mansion. Surely she had the wrong place, but there on the letter box was the exact number. Then she saw the blood-red Lamborghini parked in the driveway, she had arrived, and the fairy-tale seem to be never-ending. Isobella drove up the driveway and parked in front of the entrance. The door opened and there was Mr C in neat casual attire, holding a red rose. His silver hair shone in the sunlight, and he immediately became her knight in shining armour. Isobella wanted to run up to him and hold him tightly, before any other fair maidens whipped him away. But she knew she had to make her moves cautiously as it was only the beginning of their relationship.

As he strode towards her, Isobella noticed his beautiful leather boots, Western style; they looked really great on him, another plus she thought. He reached out and took her hand, and led her into his home. "You look lovely tonight, Isobella, as always," he said politely. "Shall we start the evening off with a glass of champagne, then I will put the music on and we will have a dance before dinner. I have everything organised." "That sounds wonderful," answered Isobella. As she started to relax with the champagne, all she could see was money and plenty of it; the home was magnificent and the furniture was of the best. Was it his? she asked herself. He must be worth a mint to own such a property, and not forgetting the blood-red Lamborghini parked out the front.

They sipped champagne together while sitting on the bar stools at the well-equipped bar. Isobella's mind slipped back to her mother for a second; Matilda would be in her element if she were here. Isobella wanted to ask many questions but the time was not right, she didn't want to jeopardise this friendship. This was a friendship that was going to last forever.

Mr C put on some music and took Isobella in his arms. They danced closely and she could smell his expensive aftershave; she hoped this moment would last forever. She was happy she had decided to wear her skintight trousers, as she could feel his body touching hers. Suddenly a bell rang, signalling that dinner was ready. "You wait here and finish your drink while I serve up," he said as he disappeared.

A few minutes had passed when Isobella heard her name called. "Come, Isobella, dinner is served." As she entered the dining room, there was a table set fit for a princess, and in the middle a candelabra was burning, which took pride of place. Silver serviette holders held beautiful starch napkins, it was a sight to behold. How could any man manage all this? But then this wasn't just any man, this man was special.

The dinner was delicious; Mr C had not only proven himself as a great host, his culinary skills were right up there at the top. After they had eaten they retired to the lounge, and there was the posh suite that Isobella had in her mind. She made her way over, kicked off her expensive shoes, lay on the suite, and dangled her legs over the side. Isobella had practised this seductive move at her home many times trying to perfect it. Her bright-red toenails stood out waiting to be noticed. Her host came over and stood behind her and gently caressed her neck. Isobella was in heaven; he certainly knew how to entertain a guest, but she was more than a guest, she was soon to be his new lover.

Mr C must have been reading her mind, as he swooped

her up and carried her to his bedroom. They both undressed each other, and the flame-red underwear set Mr C on fire. He pulled Isobella hard to him, their hot bodies touching each other. He gently kissed her shoulders then down to her breasts. Isobella ran her hands down his taut body and caressed his manly parts, arousing the passion within him. She had her prey, now she became the lioness, and pounced on him pinning him to the bed, and their bodies came together as one. He loved her passion and her hunger for sex. She was one wild woman, one he would never forget.

Isobella had the best night ever, this one she would remember. What a wonderful specimen Mr C was, his body fitted into hers like they were made for each other. She had never felt this closeness with any other man. Even the toy boy was nowhere near his calibre.

As for the city mayor, he was not even worth a mention, now that she had met Mr C. That was her old world, this was the real world.

In the morning, there on the table was a beautiful breakfast setting. Mr C was dressed in his business suit and looked a million dollars. They sat down to breakfast and Mr C said, "I had a lovely evening with you, Isobella, you are a remarkable lady; we must do this again soon."

Then it was time for them to say their goodbyes. Mr C leaned over and gave Isobella a kiss on her cheek. "I will be away for a few days, but I will contact you when I get back." They left the mansion together, Isobella in her Audi and Mr C in his Lamborghini.

As she was driving back to her home, she said to herself, It won't be long before I will be able to drive past James and Lillian's property in my blood-red Lamborghini. Just imagine James's face when he sees me waving to him from my flash car. Ideas were running wild in Isobella's head. At last she had what she deserved: a wealthy man who was handsome and charming, it was all here in this package, she would not let this go.

When Isobella came back down to earth, her heart was still racing as she thought back over the last couple of days. All her prayers were answered; no, that wasn't right, as she never prayed; all her expectations were met, she was on top of the world.

Isobella spent the days dreaming about her new life in the mansion and driving everywhere in the blood-red Lamborghini. Oh, how she would be noticed, people would be envious, and she would be the princess. More emphasis was put on the material things, Mr C was part and parcel of the package, and that he was handsome was the icing on the cake.

Days had passed by and still no phone call. Isobella was getting pretty livid, why hadn't he called her? Perhaps she could call him, but then realised she didn't have his number, but now at least, she knew where he lived. If nothing happened in the next few days she would drive out to the mansion.

Another week had passed by, so had much planning for the future. Had Isobella at last found her prince? No way was she going to let him go. Tomorrow she was going to drive out to his property; she desperately needed to see him, and could not understand why he hadn't called. He said he had enjoyed his time with her, so why no phone call? In desperation Isobella went back on to the internet into the dating site, but his profile had been removed, so that was a comforting thought. No more women could contact him, he was hers now.

The next day Isobella took her time getting dressed,

because she wanted to bowl Mr C over with her presence. When he saw her, he would have wished he hadn't waited so long between meetings. As she drove to the end of the street and was about to approach the driveway, she looked in the rear-vision mirror and here was the Lamborghini coming, her heart was racing, then there was a loud hooting so she stopped. There behind the wheel was a dark-haired woman, and she looked angry because Isobella had blocked the driveway stopping the Lamborghini from entering. In utter shock, she reversed back so the driveway was clear.

Who was this woman, what was she doing at Mr C's place, and worst of all what was she doing driving his car? This was going to be her car, no one else was allowed to drive it, least of all another woman. Isobella sat in her vehicle trying to calm down, and wondering what to do next. Then she suddenly thought of the two toothbrushes on the vanity; did he have a wife, was he being unfaithful? She waited, then saw the lady in the garden. She was not young, in fact she looked much older than Isobella. She studied her at length; could Mr C be the younger man, was she the wealthy one that was supporting him? No, this wouldn't be right because he was a businessman; perhaps she was his mother.

When she had collected her thoughts, Isobella started her car and drove off. She would give Mr C another few days and if he hadn't contacted her, there would be action. This all had to work out as she had an agenda, and that was to prove to her brother James she was in the same league as him. Not that James and Lillian belonged in any league, they were just ordinary people, but this was always in Isobella's mind, to be better than James. She still hated him, he was the one that did her out of all her inheritance. She would never forgive him.

Isobella sulked for the next few days, with millions of questions flying around in her twisted mind. The mansion, the blood-red Lamborghini, and the handsome man, this was all part of her life now, she had it all mapped out. Tomorrow was the day, she would drive to the mansion and sort things out, once and for all. If she had to, she would confront the woman she had seen driving his car, and let her know that she was having an affair with Mr C.

Confrontation day had finally arrived. Isobella dressed to kill, sporting a low neckline and figure-hugging trousers along with her stilettos; she needed to make a statement at the mansion. As she drove to the end of the street she could see the Lamborghini sitting in the driveway. Good, Mr C must be home, so Isobella prepared herself, it was her time to shine.

As she drove up the elm-covered driveway, she could see the same lady that had hooted at her a few days earlier, the one that was driving her soon-to-own Lamborghini. What was she going to say to the lady? She couldn't ask her if a Mr C lived here, as she wouldn't know who Isobella was talking about. At this moment she felt so stupid, as she didn't even have a name.

Isobella climbed out of the car and approached the lady. Thinking quickly she asked, "Could I please speak to the man of the house?"

"There is no man of the house, this is my home, I live here," she answered curtly. "Who owns that car?" asked Isobella. The lady was taken aback by these questions; who was this flashy bit, why was she here asking questions? "This is my car, why, what has it got to do with you?" she quizzed. Isobella was so shocked, no words would come out, she was dumbfounded. When she regained her composure, she had one last question. "Does anyone else drive your car?"

"I don't see that is any of your business, now please leave," she said angrily.

Poor Isobella, she hightailed it out of there as fast as she could, her mind was all over the place. She could not think straight. Who was Mr C, why had he brought her to this property? Who was this lady that owned this mansion, and the blood-red Lamborghini? Isobella's dreams were fading fast, panic and revenge were taking over. She had slept with a man in this house, who was he? My God, he was going to pay for this. No one pulled the wool over her eyes without suffering. Isobella was now in 'full revenge' mode, but where was she going to start?

She was an expert in the stalking field, as the amount of times she had stalked her previous partner was too numerous to count. She would do a twenty-four-hour surveillance on the property to see who came and went. It was a waste of time checking the number plate with the authorities as she now knew who the owner of the Lamborghini was. Other than that, she had absolutely no information whatsoever about the man who had bedded her, and this was infuriating her to the max. All was very quiet for the next twenty-four hours, no one came or went. She drove home for a few hours to freshen up, then she went back to the end of Lauderdale Street. She resumed her surveillance duty. Later that afternoon a taxi drove up to the mansion and picked someone up at the entrance. As it drove past, Isobella hid, but not before she saw that it was the dark-haired lady that she had spoken to. There seemed to be no more she could do but to drive home.

She was seething with rage. She could not get Mr C

out of her mind; even when she tried to busy herself, he was still there tormenting her. As she lay in bed that night she tried to hatch a plan to get her closer to solving her dilemma. Suddenly an idea came: she would go to the café they had met at, perhaps they might know him, he may have been there before. This she would do tomorrow.

Isobella was up and dressed at daybreak pacing around until it was time to drive to the café. As she entered the café the waitress asked, "Is it a table for two?" She had obviously remembered her and Mr C. "No, not today, just a latte for myself," replied Isobella. When the waitress came back with the coffee, Isobella asked her, "The gentleman I came here with a couple of weeks ago, do you know him, has he been here before?" "No, we don't know him, we thought you were both movie stars, as you looked the perfect couple. We all remarked how lovely it was that you came back a second time," she replied. Here was another dead end.

If Isobella was angry before, she was absolutely livid now. She walked to her car and sat and remembered their meeting at this café. Then she proceeded to drive towards her home. The road was very busy, there was traffic in every direction, but then she suddenly caught a glimpse of the blood-red Lamborghini in the far distance. Could that be Mr C? Her heart started pounding, this was the effect he had on her. One minute it was hate, then it was palpitations of her heart. There was no way she could even attempt to catch up with the Lamborghini; it was gone in a flash.

Tonight she would sit at the end of the street, outside the mansion gate, and see what was going on. About 7.30 Isobella climbed into her car and away she went. It was cold so she curled up in a blanket lying in wait. Just on dusk, lights were coming up the street, and the Lamborghini turned into the driveway, but she could not see who was in the car. She couldn't take the risk in case it was the dark-haired lady.

She would wait till the morning. Isobella must have dropped off to sleep because when she woke it was early morning, and she saw the back of the car at the end of the street disappearing out of sight. It must have come out while she was sleeping. 'Beggar,' she had missed her opportunity again. Well, it has got to come back, she told herself, so she would wait. She made herself beautiful while she waited. One hour later the Lamborghini returned and Mr C was behind the wheel. Isobella waited until he drove up the driveway, then she started her car and followed him. As she climbed out of her car, he looked surprised if not shocked to see her. What the hell is she doing here? he muttered to himself, then he had to regain his thoughts. "Hi, Isobella, I just arrived back in town yesterday. I haven't been in touch as business took longer than I anticipated. Anyhow, what are you doing out this way?" he inquired. "Oh, I saw your car in town yesterday so I knew you were back," she replied. Mr C had to think hard, but he wasn't in town yesterday, it must have been Jannie in the Lamborghini. This was getting a little close for comfort. "I have to go into town shortly, I have a meeting; come back tonight about 5.30pm," he said to Isobella. "Okay, that sounds great, see you then" was her answer, as she jumped into her car and drove away.

Mr C was shaken to the core. Thank goodness Isobella didn't come last night. He had no idea that she had been sitting in her car outside his driveway. But because she had fallen asleep, she didn't see him leaving that morning with a mystery woman in his car. Once Isobella was gone, he rushed inside and went straight to the bedroom and whipped off the sheets. He would need clean ones for tonight.

On the other side of town Isobella was swanning around the shops to find the right attire to wear tonight. Her dream was back on track. Perhaps black was the appropriate colour for tonight. Suddenly her thoughts went back to the other lady she had spoken to; perhaps she was his mother, she looked older than him. She would find out. Another matter she had to address was his name. Mr C was mysterious and romantic, but it left no clues to who he actually was, and if she had to try to trace him she needed a name, so that would also be sorted tonight.

Isobella was running up her credit card at record pace, purchasing all the flash attire she needed to lure Mr C into her web. She had told him she was financially secure, but this was not the truth. All the money she had received from her mother's estate was gone due to her expensive spending habit. But it didn't matter any more as Mr C had a wealthy mother, in her mind, and one day all this would pass on to him, so he could pay her bills. This excited Isobella; no more money worries, a blood-red Lamborghini to drive around in, a mansion and, last but not least, a handsome partner. The future looked bright through Isobella's rose-tinted Gucci glasses.

Yes, black was definitely the colour for tonight. Isobella would have a squizz around the mansion and see if she could throw some light on the other lady, as there was still a niggle in the background. Not that she could hold a candle to Isobella; she was ordinary and plain, Isobella was beautiful, she belonged to the 'society of beautiful people'.

At 5.30pm Isobella arrived at the mansion, looking the total package; she was beautiful, her figure-hugging dress hugged all the right places, she looked sensational. She felt at home in these luxurious surroundings. This was where she knew she belonged. There parked in the driveway was the blood-red Lamborghini, soon to be hers. She rang the door chime and Mr C met her with outstretched arms. "Welcome again, Isobella, you look stunning tonight." "Thank you," swooned Isobella. "Just make yourself at home while I make us a martini," said Mr C as he left the room.

Now it was time for Isobella to try to find some indication as to who the other lady was that she had met. She walked down the long hallway passing several bedrooms, including the one she and Mr C had slept in. At the end of the hallway there was a door ajar, so Isobella peeped in, only to find another bedroom. But on the wall was a large portrait of a lady, the mystery lady at last. Who was she? Isobella could not reveal to Mr C that she had spoken with her. As she turned around to leave the room, there was Mr C standing in the doorway.

"Oh, sorry for being nosy, what a lovely portrait, who is that lady?" quizzed a surprised Isobella.

Mr C had to think of an answer right on the spot. As cool as a cucumber he said, "That is my sister Jannie." "Oh, your sister, does she live here?" asked Isobella. Then her mind went into overdrive. If this was his sister then she owned everything including the blood-red Lamborghini. Where did this leave Mr C? "Please, can we have a talk?" asked Isobella. "I don't even know your name." "Come back to the drawing room, we can talk over a martini," he answered. Isobella curled up on the lounge suite feeling somewhat deflated, but she had to put all that out of her mind and enjoy the moment. "Tell me your actual name and something about yourself," asked Isobella. "Don't laugh, but I was named Conrad after my father; all my friends call me Con for short, please feel free to do the same," he replied. Isobella would certainly not be calling him Con, it had too many connotations about it. "No, I like Conrad, that's what I will call you," she said. "Please tell me about your sister, why is her portrait in the bedroom?" "That is her room, it is her wish that it is there. Come, let's dance and enjoy ourselves, let us forget the outside world. This is our world, just yours and mine, let's enjoy," he replied. With that he swept her up in his arms and held her close. She snuggled up to him, and wished he was hers totally, forever. In fact suddenly, for the first time in Isobella's life, she felt she could share a smidgen of her love with someone else. She treasured this moment. Time slipped by quickly and before they knew it, it was dark. "Come, Isobella, we must eat. Let me take you to my favourite restaurant," suggested Conrad. They finished their martinis, then Isobella slipped into her shoes, while Conrad pulled on his Western boots. Oh my God, I'm going for a ride in the Lamborghini; she was so excited. Conrad helped her climb into her seat, then he got behind the wheel and away they went. Once they hit the open road he put his foot down and she was thrown back in her seat as he accelerated. What a feeling, what a fabulous car; this was Isobella and everyone would know her soon.

They pulled up outside a lovely restaurant right on the sea front. Conrad helped her out of the car, and she could hear the waves lapping on the pier. Isobella's tight-fitting dress had crept up round her thighs, so they both made adjustments. She is one sexy 'piece', Conrad thought to himself, but for a moment his mind slipped back to Jannie; she was comforting and rich, Isobella was all for herself. He knew who he would choose over the other one, but tonight he was here to enjoy himself. As they entered the restaurant, Conrad went ahead and spoke to the head waiter. They drew glances from all the other diners as the waiter took them to a table by the window, and seated them so they could look out to sea. "Thank you, George," said Conrad with a wave of his arm. Isobella would remember George, such a common name, as he obviously knew Conrad, and if needed in the future, she would have a contact.

After dinner, they drove back to the mansion. Isobella loved this property with its tree-lined driveway, and pathway right to the front door. Conrad helped her out of the car, not bothering to adjust her dress and carried her to the entrance. He put her down while he unlocked the door, then picked her up and carried her through to the bedroom. Just to watch Isobella slip out of her slinky dress brought a rush of blood to Conrad's head. She was not young, her body was not firm like that of a younger woman, but this is what he preferred; for a woman of her age, she was doing well. Just as they climbed between the sheets, Isobella had one last question to ask: "Is this property yours?" "Partly" was the answer she got, but that was enough to satisfy her; part of all this wealth would still make him a very rich man. She could not let him know she had questioned the lady in the garden, who she now knew to be his sister Jannie.

The night was wonderful, Conrad had never met such a fierce woman in bed, and he had met plenty, but Isobella was definitely the lioness of them all. But he didn't know the extent of the hunger of this lioness. He could certainly put up with this for a week or two until Jannie returned.

The next morning Isobella awoke to the smell of toast wafting up the hallway. She showered quickly and dressed and crept out to the dining room. There seated waiting for her was her knight in shining armour; he was every bit the man of her dreams. She loved the way his eyes lit up when he saw her; they radiated a warmth that melted her heart, and made her want to be in his arms forever.

Did Isobella never for a moment think that all the women out there would love a piece of Conrad? Every woman was drawn to him, just as she was, those smiling eyes said it all. But no, he was hers; why would he look at anyone else when he could have her? This was the conceited person that she was. She had spied up the potential wealth that came with him, and thought he felt the same about her, not wealth-wise, but feeling-wise. Such selfish love had denied her of friendships in the past. Was this going to be any different, was she still a user, or was there something happening that she had never experienced before?

After breakfast Isobella excused herself, as she wanted to go home and change into something a little more comfortable. "Come back tonight, Isobella, and bring a change of clothes. We will go for a long drive tomorrow, I want to take you to someplace 'special'," said Conrad. "I will look forward to that," she said and leaned over and pecked him on the cheek. She walked to the door and said goodbye.

A long drive in the Lamborghini tomorrow, she couldn't wait. Imagine all the glances they would get, she had to look the part. The blood-red Lamborghini stood out like a sore toe, but with Conrad and Isobella in it, made it even more attractive to the outside world. She would dress appropriately for all the glances.

Before she went home, she stopped off at Guccia to buy a couple of new outfits. Conrad could not possibly see her in the same outfit twice; all her life she had followed this same pattern. This was why most of her past relationships had failed; suitors had tried to keep her in the lifestyle she was accustomed to but it was never enough. Or if they did work out, she couldn't make the decision needed for a lasting commitment. What was it that Isobella really wanted, did she really know herself, was this her problem?

Isobella asked for shop models to parade the clothes so she could see how they looked from all angles. She needed the 'wow' factor, but honestly, she had it all the time, but then classy clothes added the finishing touch to catch a man's eye. The outfit she needed to pay most attention to was the one she would be wearing while in the blood-red Lamborghini, as that was where she wanted to be noticed. To be going somewhere 'special' she had to look a million dollars. She chose black and white against the blood-red background. A white lace top with striped trousers, ones that fitted tight around her buttock area, but widened as they flowed down her long legs. To finish off the outfit, she decided to add a red scarf and red shoes to tie in with the Lamborghini.

After making her purchases, and almost maxing her credit cards, Isobella drove home, as she wanted to reflect on the situation back at the mansion. Why did Conrad's sister Jannie say she owned the property and the Lamborghini when in fact Conrad owned part of everything? Unfortunately, she could not approach this subject with Conrad; she had to be careful otherwise he would find out that she had been to the property.

That Conrad had promised to take her somewhere 'special' tomorrow sent out signals to Isobella that things were becoming serious between them. This is what she wanted to read into the relationship, and the sooner the better, as her money tree had no more leaves to drop, it was almost stripped bare.

From Conrad's point of view, he would never give up Jannie, as she was his bread and butter. She could offer him the lifestyle he had come to enjoy. His affair with Isobella was a flash in the pan, one of excitement, one which he would enjoy while it lasted, but soon it would be over. Next time Jannie went on a business trip it would be another woman and another affair. He never wanted any affairs he had to be taken seriously, they were just fleeting moments. But then Conrad had never before encountered anyone like Isobella.

The night was long and passionate, just what Conrad ordered. She was some mean lover, she had excelled in her bedroom duties and he would remember her long after their affair was finished. She was top of the 'to-be-remembered list'.

That morning after breakfast Isobella went to the wash room, showered and changed into her Lamborghini attire, the black and white with red accessories. When she walked out Conrad could not take his eyes off her as she was the pinnacle of fashion. He had noticed little aspects about her that were strange; she was a very self-first person and this worried him a little, but it was just a brief encounter, he told himself, so why worry? She would love today as he had gone to a lot of trouble to make it 'special' for her.

Isobella couldn't wait to be driven to this 'special' place she had been promised; her expectations were right up there with the best. She hoped there were going to be crowds of people around, so they could be admired. "Where are you taking me, Conrad?" she quizzed. "You will just have to wait and see, it is my favourite place," said an excited Conrad.

He helped her into the blood-red Lamborghini, and leaned over and reassured her that she would have a wonderful day, one to remember. This set Isobella's imagination into overdrive: was he going to propose to her? Of course, she would say yes, this is what she had dreamed about all her life. The city mayor was not half the calibre of her new man, and his wealth couldn't begin to compete with Conrad's.

They drove for three hours, drawing many glances from the passing public, all eager to see the couple in the blood-red Lamborghini. Isobella was in her element, this was certainly star status, but she deserved all the accolades that came her way. They drove into the heart of the city, and pulled up outside a huge modern building. A sign on the building indicated it was an art gallery. Was this where he was going to propose to her? she could think of far more romantic places than this. "Come, Isobella, I have arranged a private art showing just for the two of us. There will be no one here but you and me," announced a beaming Conrad. Where were the crowds that Isobella was expecting? She would not be noticed in this building with just Conrad and herself, she wanted an audience. "What are we going to do here?" she asked. "There is an exhibition at this gallery on one of the world's greatest modern impressionists; his name is Pino, he is Italian. His paintings are fantastic, his feelings which are of a romantic nature are expressed in his paintings. Come and have a look and tell me what you feel," said an excited Conrad. "They won't mean anything to me, I don't even like art, you can only look at it," said a selfish Isobella. She felt bitterly disappointed. Was this his idea of a wonderful surprise? It certainly wasn't hers.

All of a sudden Conrad wished it was Jannie that was here with him, she would have been so appreciative. She loved art, she would have been over the moon that he had gone to all this trouble to arrange a private showing for just the two of them.

His feelings for Isobella suddenly changed. He could not believe that someone could be so selfish, so ungrateful; he felt really hurt, as no one had treated him like this before.

"Come and sit down and I will tell you about this artist, then you will understand the love that he expresses in his paintings. When he was a young boy in Italy, all the menfolk in the village were called to war; he wanted to go but he was not of age. He stayed behind and helped the womenfolk with the heavy chores. In his spare time, he would pick up a paintbrush and paint the women and children. As he got better with his paintbrush, the young women of the village would ask him to paint their portraits. When the war was over he escaped to New York, where he was quickly snapped up as an illustrator for the cover of romantic novels. He helped launch the careers of Danielle Steel and the model Fabio. His paintings portray the elegance of women and the importance of family. Does that help stir your feelings towards his art?" inquired Conrad. "To be truthful I'm not into art, I find it boring, art is not my scene," said a disappointed Isobella.

Although Conrad was very hurt over her selfishness, he was still going to carry on and enjoy the artwork by this great artist. Isobella could sit and sulk if she chose, but he was here to enjoy himself. He walked around with his catalogue reading up about all the paintings as he viewed them. Conrad loved art, as did Jannie.

Isobella sat and sulked for a while, but as she watched Conrad, who was every woman's dream, admiring the art-work, she suddenly woke to the fact that she had been self-ish and had put on a childish display. She didn't want to lose him; she had run up her credit cards nearly to the max, to look the perfect picture for him; who was going to pay for these? He was her ticket to be debt free. She had to try to make amends! She got up and walked over to Con-rad. "I'm sorry, I was selfish, let me join you and you can try and explain the paintings to me," said a sorry Isobella as she linked her arm in his. "It is sad that you don't share a love of art, the other women I have brought here have loved it, that's why I arranged the private showing," said Conrad.

Isobella flinched; did she hear right, did he say he had brought other women to this gallery? But this was meant to be 'special', for her. She was furious; suddenly the old jealousy was back and rearing its ugly head. She had to bite her tongue, otherwise she would have let fly; she had done enough damage already today. Now she had to work hard to get Conrad on her side again. She couldn't lose him. Why was she like this? But if she had taken the time to reflect back on her life, and remember all the lies and all the people she had hurt, perhaps she could have redeemed herself, long before it got to this stage.

As they left the gallery, Conrad walked around and helped her into the Lamborghini. It didn't take long before the smiles came back on Isobella's face. People were every-where admiring the car and the couple that had just got into it. Isobella felt important again, now that she had escaped that boring old art gallery. But she was too full of herself to notice that Conrad had somewhat cooled off. Not a lot was said on the way home, but Isobella had closed her eyes and was in her own little fairy-tale world. Tonight, she would make it up to Conrad, she would give him another night to remember and all would be forgiven.

Conrad had other ideas. He wanted to get rid of Isobella, the sooner the better. He was sad it had to end like this, but for the first time he saw her for what she was, and he felt it was time for him to move on before his secret life ran into problems. Tonight he had to leave town for business, that's what he would tell her when they arrived back at the mansion. Jannie wasn't due back for another ten days, so if Isobella came to the mansion there would be no one there. He would go to their out-of-town bach until Jannie came home. He had left no traces that Isobella could follow up on. She would give up after ten days.

But if Conrad thought it was going to be that easy, he was in for one big surprise.

After Conrad pulled up in the Lamborghini he parked it at the front entrance as he would be using it later. He let Isobella in the front door and said he would be there in a minute as he had a phone call to make. As she walked in the door, for the first time she noticed all the paintings on the wall; she hadn't seen them before, as art meant nothing to her. She was looking for more expensive things, and art was not one of them, but the Lamborghini and the mansion, that was another story.

As Conrad entered the lounge, he looked frustrated. "Isobella, I have had a call from work, I am leaving the country tonight, so I have only got an hour to get ready; I'm sorry but you will have to leave. As soon as I get back I will call you." "Oh Conrad, I was going to make everything right between us tonight," she said, sounding disappointed. "Give me your phone number so I can call you." "No, I can't do that as I have a new phone and number coming next week; when I get it I'll give it to you," replied Conrad.

Isobella sensed an air of 'standoff' between them. She didn't want it to be like this before he left. She went up to him and held him tight and pressed her body into his. "Come to bed now," she begged. How could he refuse, this was going to be the last time, and he had to admit she certainly knew how to treat a man. She was always going to linger in his mind well after the affair had ended. They made love, she was good, never had he met such an amorous lover. It was going to be sad to say goodbye to their bedroom manoeuvres, but it was time to move on. Conrad could see problems on the horizon if this didn't end now. She would have to forget him and put it down to a memorable experience, just like he was going to do.

They said their goodbyes as they both got into their respective vehicles. Isobella drove off first and parked at the end of the street, as she wanted to see Conrad and the blood-red Lamborghini drive by. How she wanted both these items.

Isobella was disappointed that nothing had eventuated from the 'special' day that Conrad had arranged. She was hoping for a commitment, but all she got was a few hours at a boring art gallery. And the bombshell, 'other women I have brought here have loved it'. Did he think I was like every other woman? He would soon learn that I was different.

Nearly a week had passed and Isobella hadn't received a call from Conrad. She wondered when he would be back, as she was actually missing him. Why was she feeling like this? It had never happened before! She could always move on, but not this time. Her head was spinning, he was haunting her. Was this the feeling of love? She had only ever loved herself, until she met Conrad. Please ring me, she kept repeating in her head.

After a week it got too much for Isobella, so she drove out to the mansion, but the Lamborghini was not there and the mansion was all locked up. It was driving her mad, she had to contact him, but how? She decided to wait another few days then drove out again, but with the same result.

Meanwhile Conrad had contacted Jannie and persuaded her to come down to the bach for a couple of weeks, so they could swim and surf together, as he was missing her. This she agreed to do, as she loved Conrad, he was a warm comforting person. This would give him roughly three weeks away from the mansion. Isobella would have given up by then.

Two weeks had now passed and Isobella had driven to the mansion four times. She was getting angry now, as Conrad promised to ring and give her his new phone number, but this had not happened. She sat down and tried to work out how she could contact him, but she had no leads. Who would know him?

Then she had a thought: the restaurant by the sea, which was his favourite dining place. The waiter George knew him. She got into her car and drove out to the restaurant. As she walked in, there was George showing some people to their seats. She waited until he was free then she approached him. He remembered her, but seemed awkward, and could not look her in the eye. "George, the gentleman I dined with here a couple of weeks ago, do you know him?" "I'm sorry, but no, I don't," replied George. "But he called you George as if he knew you," said Isobella. "I saw him talking to you as we came in, he said this was his favourite restaurant." What could George do but tell the truth.

"I have never seen him before, but he asked me to act as if I knew him, and he slipped me a note." "Thank you, George," said Isobella, and she left.

Why would Conrad do that? He loved her, and now she thought she loved him. They were an item, she needed him, how were her bills going to be paid? It was because of him she had spent the money she didn't have, it was all Conrad's fault. Back to the mansion she went, but still no Lamborghini. Had something happened to him? Isobella tried to keep herself occupied, but her mind was going round and round in circles. She thought by now she would have been driving past James and Lillian's place in her blood-red Lamborghini showing off to them. This made her even more angry thinking about it, but it would happen, she told herself, karma happened!

By now a month had passed and still Isobella wasn't giving up. She drove to town and stopped at her Guccia shop to buy a new outfit, one that would make her look like the princess that she was. This would be her last purchase, as her credit cards were maxed out. She had to forsake the matching scarf, the cards were spent. But after today she would have no more worries. She drove home and slipped into her new outfit; it was stunning, the mirror never told lies; she was Bartholomew and Matilda's favourite child. This she would never forget.

Now she was on her way to the mansion, Isobella was welling up with excitement, surely Conrad would be back by now. As she reached the end of the street, there up the driveway at the entrance of the mansion was the Lamborghini; he was back. She climbed out of her car, did a few last-minute adjustments, then walked up and rang the door chime. She waited with bated breath; in a minute she would be in Conrad's arms.

The door opened and there stood the same lady she had encountered on one other visit. This was the lady in the portrait, this must be Conrad's sister Jannie. Isobella was stuck for words, but it was Jannie who spoke first. "Can I help you? I remember you, you have been here before. What can I do for you this time?" Jannie wondered what this beautiful woman was doing here again. "Oh. I've come to see your brother," stuttered Isobella. "My brother is overseas," replied Jannie. "When will he be back?" inquired Isobella. Jannie thought this was strange, as her brother actually lived overseas, she didn't know when he was due back. "Oh, I don't know, he hasn't said anything about returning," said Jannie. Poor Isobella was in shock. Conrad had not even told his sister when he was coming back. "Could you please give me his phone number, I need to contact him," said a desperate Isobella. "Just a minute, I will get it for you," and away Jannie went. She began to wonder why this woman wanted to contact her brother. He already had a partner, and it wasn't a female. How would these two know each other? She found his number and brought it out and gave it to Isobella. She thanked Jannie and got in her car and drove away. If she was upset before, now she was furious. 'That bloody Conrad, what was he playing at? I'll fix him when I get him on the phone,' thought a seething Isobella.

As she drove back home, her mind was raging like a wild bull. Then she realised she didn't even know what country she had to ring, although Jannie had put a country code before the number. But what country was he in? The code meant nothing to Isobella. Never mind, she would soon find out. She waited until 7.00pm and picked up her phone and started dialling the number. She was angry as well as excited, but just to hear Conrad's voice again, she couldn't wait.

Suddenly there was a muffled voice at the end of the line. "Who is that?" "This is Isobella, is that you, Conrad?" she asked. "No, this is not Conrad, it is 3.00am in the morning. You have got the wrong number," then bang went the receiver. Poor Isobella, she was beside herself, perhaps she had rung the wrong number, she would try again. "Who the hell is there?" said a muffled voice again. "It's me, Isobella," she said. "Are you the person who just rung me? Don't ring again, do you hear me?" then a bang.

Where to from here? Isobella checked the numbers she had been given and the numbers she had rung and they were the same. She decided to work out the time differences and she would ring again later. When it was 8.30am over wherever, she picked up the phone again and rang. "Hello, this is Isobella. I am sorry for ringing you earlier this morning but I am looking for Conrad," she said. "I don't know a Conrad. How did you get my number?" he asked. "Your sister Jannie gave it to me," replied Isobella. "I asked her for her brother's number and this what she gave me." "Yes, I am Jannie's brother, but my name is Stephen, not Conrad, and I live here in Detroit," he said. "But have you been out to New Zealand lately?" asked Isobella. "No, I left New Zealand fifteen years ago and have not been back since. Why?" "So you don't have a brother called Conrad?" she asked. "No, there is just Jannie and myself left in our family." "Is Jannie married?" asked Isobella. "Heavens no, she doesn't need anyone to support her, she is a wealthy lady, her husband left her well off when he passed away. Why all these questions about this Conrad?" Isobella didn't want to have to explain, she felt empty and betrayed. Who this man was with whom she had slept, she had no idea, and she hated herself for this. "It's a long story, but thank you for your help," and she hung up.

For the first time in her life, Isobella had met her match.

There was someone out there who had taken advantage of her, and there was nothing she could do. She had lost control, never had anything like this happened before, she had always been the one that called the shots. Then she remembered her credit cards; who was going to pay them off, now that she had maxed them to their limits? Her life was an absolute mess.

Isobella was all out to get revenge on this Conrad character who had betrayed her. There was no blood-red Lamborghini, no mansion and now no handsome man; those dreams were over.

She thought hard and fast as to what to do next. She would go back to the mansion and confront Jannie. This imposter had to be exposed, as she felt utterly disgusted with herself. She had given herself to someone, but who was he? For all the money she had spent, there were meant to be rewards, instead all she was left with was shame and debt ... plenty of it.

Isobella decided to drive out to the mansion to confront Jannie. She would tell her that she had been in her house with Conrad, and she knew there was a portrait of Jannie in the bedroom, because she had seen it there. Also, the plush suite was against the back-lounge wall. Then she tried to remember what paintings were on the lounge wall, but her mind went blank. She never took any notice because they weren't her thing, but she wished now she had been more vigilant. All she had thought about was the mansion and the blood-red Lamborghini, as these spelt wealth and happiness.

On the Friday, Isobella drove out to the mansion and saw the Lamborghini in the driveway. Perhaps Conrad was back, and the excitement came rushing back. As she got out of the car she saw Jannie in the garden. She called to her: "Hi, Jannie, could I please talk to you?" "Just a minute," called Jannie. With this she came over to Isobella's car. "What can I do for you? I had a call from Stephen and he said you called him and woke him up in the early hours of the morning. He still doesn't know what you wanted. Who is Conrad?" Isobella didn't know where to start. "Conrad told me he was your brother. I saw your portrait in the bedroom hanging on the wall, and asked who you were. He said you were Jannie, his sister." "Where did you say my portrait was hanging?" quizzed Jannie. "In the bedroom on the blank wall," Isobella replied. Jannie began to wonder what was going on with this flashy-looking woman. Then she thought back to their first meeting and all the questions that she asked. Who was she? "My portrait is on the lounge wall, not the bedroom wall," said Jannie. "No, it was on the bedroom wall," said an indignant Isobella. With this, Jannie asked Isobella to come into the house, and took her into the lounge. There was the portrait on the lounge wall. "But all the furniture has been moved around," Isobella replied.

"I think you had better leave," Jannie said. Someone must have told her about the mansion, but she is all mixed up. She watched her drive down the driveway. I can't wait until Mason comes home and I tell him about this strange woman.

Life was going from bad to worse for Isobella, but bad things had happened many times before, this was not the first. Now she felt a complete fool, as well as used; she had lost control, never had life been so complicated. She thought back for a moment: her toy boy had moved on, the city mayor was past tense and her brother James wouldn't want to know her after what she had done to him.

All the money from Matilda's estate was gone. Isobella had squandered it on clothes, shoes and having a good time. But as always, she never looked to the future, she lived for the moment. It was different for her now, as there were no backstops, no more family money to fall back on. It looked like she was going to have to go back to work and earn money. This was when she had flashbacks to Matilda; if only she hadn't changed her will, then she would still have money; she couldn't let go of the feeling that Matilda had betrayed her.

Meanwhile back at the mansion Jannie was welcoming Mason home. She couldn't wait to tell him about the strange lady that was here, asking for a Conrad. "You know, Mason, she even told me my portrait was on the bedroom wall, so I asked her in and showed her it was on the lounge wall, then she said the furniture had been moved. This is the third time she has been here, and I'm a little worried. I told her not to come back."

Conrad ... Mason was upset, as he thought she would have given up by now. He was angry that she had been pestering Jannie. He praised his own actions for removing Jannie's portrait and rearranging the furniture. It was only when Isobella poked her nose down the end of the hallway and saw the portrait, and asked who it was, that caught him by surprise, so he quickly thought to say it was a portrait of his sister.

Conrad had to admit his time with Isobella was fun while it lasted, and that was all he was out for, a good time, not a commitment. He had actually used her and was now ready to cast her aside. Perhaps it was fate that brought them together. They were two of a kind, but at this point in time Conrad was out in front. Had the femme fatale spider met the male funnel-web?

Isobella was back at the job she knew best, the only job she knew, and that was as a waitress. She had applied for a position at a dinky little café away from the area she knew, as she didn't want people seeing her back working. She had told everybody about her inheritance and that she would never have to work again, but this money was never going to last, especially at the pace she was spending. It was nose to the grindstone for her now, as there was debt to start paying back. Occasionally at night she would go on the computer, to the dating scene to see if Conrad popped up, but no, he hadn't. Isobella was still hurting about going to bed with a complete stranger; who was he?

Then one day at the café, there was huge excitement among the staff. "Come and have a look at this, it's fabulous," they called out to Isobella, so she went to the window to have a look. There parked outside the café was the blood-red Lamborghini. Her heart pounded as she thought of Conrad, she could not get him out of her mind. "Who got out of the car?" asked Isobella. No one had seen who parked the car. Isobella was then called to serve customers, and when she came back it was gone. This reignited her thoughts of revenge and love, both at the same time. The two passions were entwined. For the first time in her life she had to admit that she felt love for someone other than herself. This was a first.

Isobella had the weekend off from the café, so spent her time browsing the shops, doing what she did best. She had refrained from buying clothes, until her credit cards were reduced to a more manageable level. She didn't need flash dresses as she was not dating, she was still hurting over Conrad.

When she went back to work on the Monday morning, the café was abuzz with excitement. "Isobella, the blood-red Lamborghini came back, and out climbed the most fashionable couple. They came into the café and ordered a latte, and sat and chatted together, they looked like film stars, and were the envy of everyone. He was one good-looking dude, and was wearing the most fab cowboy boots." Isobella was in shock, could this be Conrad? "Was the woman with him dark-haired and quite short?" she inquired. "No, she was tall and blonde," the girls answered. Isobella could hardly hide back her tears. That must have been Conrad, but who was this other woman? Did he have a new lover? Her heart was broken; why did he stop seeing her?

That night as she lay in bed thinking over her time with Conrad, Isobella suddenly realised that she had over-looked something. If there was only Jannie and her brother, who lived in Detroit, left in the family, then how could Jannie be Conrad's sister? She sat upright in bed and the alarm bells started ringing. Who the hell was Conrad? There was something sinister going on here, and Isobella could certainly identify with this word as she had been in these situations before, with her brother James. It was not a nice place to be, especially when the tables were turned.

Tomorrow after work Isobella would go home and change, and drive out to the mansion just on dark and find out what was going on. She had to know!

As Isobella drove up the driveway to the mansion she could see the Lamborghini parked at the front entrance.

Beside it was another vehicle, one she had not seen

before, a jet-black Ferrari. She didn't know how she was going to tackle the situation, she would just let it unfold on its own. She walked up to the entrance, then stopped as she could hear music playing, the same music she and Conrad had danced to. She regained her composure and rang the door chime. A few minutes later the door opened, and there stood Conrad. He looked like he had seen a ghost and just froze. Isobella pushed past him and went to where the music was playing. There in a flimsy nightdress was a woman dancing with a glass of champagne in her hand. She was calling to Conrad, "Who was that? Come, darling, I want another dance." Then she stopped when she saw Isobella standing there. "Who is this, Mason, what is she doing here?" demanded the mystery woman. "Yes, Mason, what am I doing here?" mimicked Isobella. "You have some explaining to do; start now." "Please, Isobella, just leave, I will ring you tomorrow. I will explain everything then," said Conrad. "No, explain now, or I will," snapped Isobella. "Oh, I see you have removed Jannie's portrait again, is it in the bedroom?" and with this she walked up the hallway and there on the bedroom wall was the portrait. When she came back into the lounge, the other woman was gone, she could hear the car speeding down the driveway.

They stood looking at each other, neither could say a word. Isobella's heart was racing, whether in anger or excitement, she was confused, but in spite of everything she still wanted him.

"Right, Conrad. I will tell you what I know: you are not Jannie's brother. Who are you?" Conrad's mind was racing, what lies could he tell now? He didn't want to jeopardise his relationship with Jannie, otherwise he would have nothing. If she kicked him out he would have nowhere to go. He didn't love her as such, but they were compatible, and enjoyed each other's company. She was kind and generous to him. But if she knew there were other women, he would be out on his ear. What could he tell Isobella? She was one dangerous woman, one he wished he had never met. He had to come clean.

"Jannie and I are partners, we have been together now for six years. She is a kind person, and is ten years older than me. Because of this, the passion is not there, so I seek other ladies from time to time, but she does not know of this," said a guilty Conrad. Isobella thought hard and fast about the situation. "If I can still have you as my lover, and you can be a companion to Jannie, then this will be our secret," she replied. Conrad looked surprised, this was not what he wanted, he just wanted her to go away. But he could see at this stage it was never going to happen, so he would have to agree to this arrangement in the meantime. "Only one other rule: no more women, just you, me and Jannie; this will be a three-way relationship. If there is anyone else, you will be exposed," said a smug Isobella.

Now she had him trapped, he was hers once again.

Conrad and Isobella were both predators, now that they had found each other it was a case of who was the strongest, who would survive! Once again Isobella had spun her web and into it she had drawn another vulnerable prey.

It so turned out that Jannie was away on a business trip for a week so the coast was clear for Isobella to make some demands. She would come back to the mansion tomorrow after work and stay the night with Conrad, then they could put a plan in place, as to how they were going to handle the situation. While Isobella was bursting at the seams with excitement, Conrad was filled with anger, his whole deceitful world was now confined to just Jannie and Isobella. He knew how dangerous she was, that is why he wanted to finish with her, hoping she would just disappear and that would be the end. Oh, but not so with Isobella, she deserved the best in life ... it owed her, as he was about to find out. Would this beautiful couple one day self-destruct?

The next afternoon when Isobella finished work she went straight to her favourite lingerie store. Tonight she must look seductive for Conrad, now that he was hers again. She had whittled her debt down, so now she could start spending. She took her time to select something perfect, a beautiful lacy negligee; it was very expensive, but he was worth every penny. Then she slipped next door to Guccia to buy a little black dress, something fitting, something special. She was so happy to have him back in her life that she would go the ends of the earth to keep it that way. If Jannie was not a good lover, then she would fill that void. And to be driven around in the Lamborghini, that was the icing on the cake, she would make sure they drove places so she could be seen.

That night she drove to the mansion, to her place of sanctuary, to where her new life would begin with Conrad, even if it meant sharing him with Jannie. She was forgetting that Jannie was the owner of all she desired, that she and Conrad were just bystanders.

Conrad was not his bright self when he greeted her, and showed her into the home. There was no suggestion of dancing or even a martini. They sat down at the dining table, and Conrad wanted to know how the relationship was going to work, what did Isobella have in mind? "When Jannie is away, I will come here and stay with you, this will be my home when she is absent. In between times you can come to my home and sleep with me," said a happy Isobella.

Conrad was furious; here was a woman giving him the ultimatum, my way or no way, but he realised he had no choice but to play along, or there would be devastating consequences for him. He would lose Jannie and all the privileges that went with her. He couldn't risk this.

"I will give up my job," she told Conrad. "No, don't do that, I will be away on business a lot of the time, so you need an interest," he quickly replied. No way did he want her hanging around Jannie's mansion while she was away, or for that matter while he was there. He would feel stifled, along with the worry that came with her. As long as he could have her for his pleasure without any commitments, then this would be different, as she was an exciting lover. Now that she came with conditions, this frightened him as he had not been in this position before.

This was the beginning of one very lopsided affair, one he wished he had never begun. Isobella took him in her arms and held him closely; she could feel his body close to hers, but all Conrad felt was a woman of stone, one who was in total control. As the night went by he started to panic; what was going to happen at bedtime, would he be able to perform, or had worry become his worst fear.? This was a predicament he had never had to face before. But worse was to come: Isobella had another surprise waiting in the wings.

"Tonight, we are going to sleep in Jannie's bedroom, now that I am the second lady of the mansion," she said excitingly. "No, that is not going to be a happening thing, no one sleeps in Jannie's room, it is special for her," said a shocked Conrad. "Well, get used to it, because this is going to be our room when I am staying here," she demanded. Poor Conrad, things were going from bad to worse. How the hell did I get into this situation? he asked himself.

As bedtime neared, Isobella made her way to Jannie's room. This was hers now, the four-poster bed looked inviting. "Come to bed, Conrad, I'm waiting," she called. "I'll be there in a moment!" he yelled. He was furious: here was Isobella breaking all the rules that he had in place. No way should she be in this room, she was nowhere near Jannie's calibre. As he reached the door he paused and said, "Isobella, this is Jannie's bed, let us go to our bed." "No, I am tucked up here now, and I'm comfortable, besides I love this four-poster bed. Come, I am ready for you". She could give orders as she was now the second mistress of the mansion.

Conrad had no choice, but it was so against his grain to have to obey a woman, especially Isobella. He took his time as he made his way to the bed, and as he climbed in, he felt an arm reaching for him. He just wanted to turn his back and go to sleep, but she had other ideas. Tonight she wanted to please Conrad, and as hard as she tried, he could not respond. It was wrong for him to be in this bed with someone else. "What is wrong, you seem distant tonight? I'm trying to please you but there is no response," questioned an unhappy Isobella. "I'm sorry but this is Jannie's room, let us go to our room," he said again. That will be the day, Isobella thought to herself. This is my room when 'she' was not here; I will leave Conrad to sulk, tomorrow will be another day, he will come around. They both turned their backs and went to sleep.

In the deep of night, she reached out for Conrad but the bed was empty, she was there alone. She got up and crept down the hallway, and found him in their bed sound asleep. She stood for a minute, then walked over and slide in beside him; his arm was out of the bedcovers so she put it around her and went to sleep. When Conrad woke in the morning he was surprised to find her lying next to him. "What are you doing in here?" he asked. "I found you here on your own, so decided to join you," replied Isobella. "Time for breakfast, then work for you," he said as he bounced out of bed before she made any advances. Conrad cooked breakfast for her while she showered and got dressed. He couldn't wait to see her drive out the driveway. Isobella leaned over and gave him a peck on the cheek as she was leaving the mansion. "See you tonight," she called.

The first job Conrad did was whip the sheets off Jannie's bed and replace them with clean ones. That was it, tonight he would put his foot down, never again would she enter Jannie's room.

Isobella wanted to surprise and impress the girls at the café where she worked. She told them she had a special man, and she would bring him for a latte at the weekend, but they were not to let on they knew her. She was to be just another customer to them. The main reason being she didn't want Conrad to know she was just a waitress. They all agreed to play Isobella's game, as they wanted to see her 'special' man.

When Isobella went home to the mansion that night, Conrad had cooked dinner. She was delighted. They sat and had a wine before dinner, then ate. After cleaning up they curled up on the settee and watched a movie. Conrad had to pick the right time to break the sad news, that he had been called away to work on Sunday, so Isobella would have to go back to her home. He promised to call her when he got back. "Tonight we are sleeping in our bedroom, this is where 'our memories' are, and I insist we bed here," he said masterfully. Isobella decided to cut him some leeway, so agreed, as what he said — 'our memories' — made her feel special. Perhaps she had been a bit keen to try to rule the roost. That night things were almost back to normal in bed; Isobella was happy, but Conrad was living a nightmare.

Today was Saturday, so Isobella suggested they go to a little café that she knew, that had great lattes. Into the Lamborghini they climbed and away they drove, with Conrad following her directions. They pulled up outside the little café, and Isobella asked that they just sit for a few minutes. She could see eyes peering through the windows to look at the blood-red Lamborghini and to see who was going to get out. Conrad climbed out and walked around and helped Isobella out. She was dressed beautifully, and when the girls recognised her there were screams of delight. Here she was with that gorgeous man they had seen a couple of weeks ago.

Into the café walked Conrad followed by Isobella, and asked to be seated by the window. The girls pulled out the chairs for them to sit down, and left them to sort out what they wanted. They gathered in the preparation area and couldn't stop talking about Isobella. Then there was nearly a fight to see who was going to take their orders. They ordered lattes, and sat chatting, because tomorrow Conrad was leaving on business, and she was returning to her own home. As they left they thanked the staff, then walked over and climbed into the Lamborghini, and there were the girls all lined up peeping through the café window. Isobella gave them a final wave, and away they went. She could just imagine what the girls were going to say on Monday when she went back to work.

That night Conrad cooked dinner for them; he was amazing, he could whip up a meal in no time. This was another point that Isobella loved about him. She had never had to cook a meal. Now they had to make plans as Jannie would probably be back before Conrad returned. "I will call you when I get back, I don't want you to come to the mansion while Jannie is here," pointed out Conrad. He was pleased to be getting away from Isobella. How was he going to carry on this affair? He had no intention of being with one woman for any length of time, other than with Jannie. But he had met a self-centred woman who could be very dangerous if things didn't go her way. He had been lucky with his affairs up until now.

After another successful night, only from Isobella's side of the story, she packed her clothes, as she was leaving the mansion. Her stay here was cut short because of Conrad's work. They said their goodbyes at the entrance then Conrad walked Isobella to her car. "Work hasn't said how long I will be, so don't worry if it is a week or two," he said. "I hope it's not two weeks, I'll miss you so much," she said as she reached over and kissed him, then climbed into her car and drove down the driveway amid the elms.

Conrad was relieved to see the back of her car and Isobella. He was petrified things were getting out of hand. He decided it was now time to secure his future with Jannie. He would propose to her before it was too late. He could see his lifestyle being eroded by Isobella, so he would have to act fast before all was lost. His meetings with Laura were safe as she didn't want her husband Michael to know, so it suited both parties. Why couldn't Isobella be like that, but of course she was a free spirit with no attachments.

On Monday morning when Isobella turned up at the café, she was the envy of all her work colleagues.

Questions were flying in all directions: where did she meet him, was he rich, was the Lamborghini his and many more ... Isobella told them all they were an item, and yes, he was rich and he lived in a mansion on Lauderdale Street. She didn't tell them they had met on the internet on a dating site and that he was two-timing several women.

# 9

# A Change of Fortune for Isobella



Isobella received a phone call one evening asking her to call into the Guccia store on Fifth Avenue at her earliest convenience. This was the store where she bought all her clothes. She wondered what was wrong, had the credit card rejected her last purchase? There was nothing she could do till the morning; she was truly worried.

She turned up at the Guccia store the next morning, and was shown into the manageress's office. She was asked to sit down. "Hi, Isobella, I am Natalie, this is my store. Isobella, we love the way you wear our clothes, you are a walking model, especially for the mature women, and we would like to know if you would think about coming to work for us, and model our clothes instore for our clients. It will be a full-time position, and a good remuneration package goes with this job should you accept it. We love seeing you walk out of the store in our clothes, you look stunning." Isobella was shocked, what could she say? In her wildest dreams she could never imagine this happening. "I would love to work here," she answered. "Would you be able to start in a fortnight, would that give you enough time to get sorted?" asked Natalie. "Yes, a fortnight will be fine," replied Isobella.

As she left the store she was over the moon. At last she would be working in an environment where she would have job satisfaction, wearing the clothes she loved, and modelling for the clients. Nothing could be more rewarding for her, this was a dream come true.

This new position took her mind away from Conrad for the time being. She still came first and foremost, the other items including Conrad were secondary. First she would have to notify the café that she was leaving, she would miss the girls, but greener pastures called. This was the end of her menial job, she was climbing the ladder to a better and brighter future.

Today was Isobella's first day at Guccia. She was excited to be working among all the beautiful clothes that she so admired, and loved to wear. Just to be able to walk around and touch the creations as they hung in the cubicles on display was exciting in itself. This was where she belonged, among beautiful things. If mature ladies wanted to see the clothes modelled before they bought, then Isobella was their contact person. This was a great sales ploy on Natalie's behalf, as anything Isobella wore looked fabulous, so hopefully the clients would think they would look the same. This was why she was employed, she was a draw-card, a huge asset for the business.

In her first week, she met many influential ladies, as this was where the 'who's who' shopped. Of course, most of the clients were monied women as the clothes weren't cheap. Only the rich, or women like herself who loved clothes and didn't mind running up debt on their credit cards, shopped at this store. Sometimes clients would bring their partners along to watch Isobella model potential purchases. Of course, she loved the limelight and the limelight loved her. So did the menfolk that came; they looked past the garments and visualised the sexy model underneath the clothes, wondering if she was available.

In all her excitement Isobella realised it was nearly a month since she had heard from Conrad. It was not such a painful wait as there was so much else going on in her life. She still didn't have his phone number, so she couldn't call him; she would give him another week.

The following week at Guccia, on the Tuesday morning, into the shop walked Jannie and Conrad, hand in hand. Natalie came up to Isobella and asked her to pay special attention to this couple as they were valuable clients. When they saw Isobella they both acknowledged her; Natalie was surprised that she knew this couple, she would ask her about them later. "Please may I be of any assistance to you?" asked Isobella. Conrad was still reeling from the shock of seeing her working in this store, as he had been back for a couple of weeks and not bothered to contact her. "Yes, I am looking for a lovely dress to wear on a special occasion," said Jannie. "Mason has asked me to marry him, I'm so happy."

This sent Isobella into a spin, but she could not let this interfere with her work, she loved her job. She was utterly shocked that Conrad had asked Jannie to marry him; she had hoped it would be her privilege one day. What was he thinking? Jannie couldn't hold a candle to her, but she hadn't worked out that Jannie was well off; she had very little to offer, only herself.

Natalie came up to Jannie and said, "We have a new shipment of fashions coming next week, there will be some beautiful items; wait until then, you will have a larger range to choose from. Is there any hurry to buy today?" "Oh no, we have two months before our big day," replied Jannie. Conrad's big strong shoulders had slumped through this ordeal, and he couldn't wait to get out of the store.

Now he would have to contact Isobella or she might come out to the mansion. She watched them leave the shop, and saw Conrad helping Jannie climb into the Lamborghini. How envious she was, not of Jannie but of the mansion, the Lamborghini and Conrad. Just how many names did he have? He told her he was Conrad, but in truth he was Mason. Isobella only knew him as Conrad, so this is what she would continue to call him.

As Isobella stood and watched them leave, Natalie came over and asked her how she knew Jannie and Mason. "Oh, we go a long way back, I knew Mason many years ago," she said. "He is the most handsome man I have ever met; Jannie is so lucky, but then she is a lovely person. I might have stolen him for myself, he is the most talked about guy around town," Natalie admitted. Isobella was so infuriated, she wanted him all the more after this comment. She wished she could tell Natalie they were lovers, but she valued her job too much.

That night Conrad rang Isobella. "Come and stay with me tonight," she pleaded. "No, I can't come tonight, Jannie is having friends over, so I am tied up," replied Conrad. "Just make sure you come tomorrow night, I will be expecting you," and with this she hung up. Isobella was so jealous, she wished it was her partying at the mansion.

How was Conrad going to explain to Jannie that he had to go out tonight. After thinking about it for some time he came up with a plan. He would tell Jannie he was going to a meeting, he would visit Isobella and make her happy, then through the night he would come back home to the mansion. He would leave a note with Isobella explaining why he had left.

Isobella couldn't wait for Conrad to arrive and take her in his arms. She had changed into her silk night attire so she could feel his body against hers. He had never been to her house before, she did wonder what he would think as it was not near the calibre of what he had come from. As Conrad pulled up at the gate he noticed that all the houses in the street were of similar vintage, neat and tidy, not what he was used to, but then in reality, it was better than what he would have if Jannie wasn't supporting him. He knocked at the door. "Come in," Isobella called in a demanding voice. Suddenly he wished he could turn around and drive away and not be here, just the tone in her voice was enough to make him feel like this. But he was trapped, he was here to fulfil a duty, and this he must do as best he could. "Oh Conrad, I have missed you so much, when you came into the shop my heart skipped a beat, I just wanted to touch you. Please hold me in your arms and love me," she pleaded. She put her arms around him and held him close, feeling his body touching hers. He was such a hunk of a man and when she gazed into his eyes, she melted. "Come to bed, I've waited so long for this, I was jealous seeing you with Jannie, I wished it was me there with you instead of her," she said as she led him to her bedroom.

Did she always have to bring his Jannie into their conversation? He hated this; why couldn't she forget her when they were together? Conrad tried to be as loving as he could, it was nowhere near his best performance, but he had made Isobella happy, that was the best he could hope for. She talked about her job at the store and how she modelled the clothes for the clients, and they all liked her, it was a conversation all about Isobella but that was par for the course. He was hoping for the 'tittle-tattle' to stop and for her to fall off to sleep so he could leave the note on the pillow. Eventually she did drop off and Conrad took her arm from around him, slipped out of bed, left the note and off he went.

In the morning when Isobella woke, she reached over to cuddle into Conrad but he was not there. She thought he must be getting her breakfast so she lay there rethinking the night's events. Oh, to have him back in her arms where he belonged, she felt on top of the world. Then the sudden realisation that in two months' time he would be married to Jannie, she felt anger. As she moved over to Conrad's side of the bed she felt something cold against her cheek. There was the note; she picked it up and read it: 'Sorry, Isobella, I had to leave early, work called me again, I will be away for another week at least. Enjoyed our night together, will be in touch, Conrad.' Isobella felt let down once again. He wasn't even able to spend one whole night with her. She was furious.

Just as well work was going along great, it took her mind off Conrad. She loved working and mixing with influential people. She was an asset to the store, the profits had gone up remarkably since she was employed, and more and more husbands were accompanying their wives to Guccia. There was more demand for Isobella to model the clothes, it was several times a day now.

One day as she was dressing up the windows she saw a familiar face coming through the door. She realised it was Lillian, her sister-in-law, James's wife. Surely she wouldn't shop here, thought Isobella. Lillian is such a plain person, she didn't tend to dress in trendy fashions; these clothes would be too upmarket for her. Natalie went over and offered to help her. "I am looking for something special for a friend's wedding," said Lillian. "Certainly," said Natalie. "Where is the wedding to take place? Then we can go from there." "At my friend's home, it is a garden wedding to be held at Lauderdale Street," replied Lillian. "Oh, is it Jannie McIntyre's wedding?" asked Natalie. "Yes, we are old school friends, she is a lovely person," said Lillian. "It will be quite a posh wedding, her husband left her very well off when he passed away. Her new man, Mason, they tell me is quite some guy, I haven't met him but my husband James knows him."

Isobella heard this all from the store window, and nearly fell through the glass, she felt her knees buckle and she felt faint. She wanted to yell at the top of her voice to Lillian, 'This is not true, you don't know them, they are my life, not yours!' "I will sort some fashions for you to try on, although we do have a store model if you would like to see the clothes on her," said Natalie. "No, it's all right I will try them on myself, I know what I like," Lillian replied. "If you don't find something special, I have a new shipment coming in next week, there will be plenty of fabulous fashions to choose from," said a helpful Natalie. "Oh, that will be great, I will wait till then, thank you for your help," replied Lillian. She then left the store.

Isobella could not believe what she had just witnessed. How the hell did James know Conrad, and to think Lillian was a friend of Jannie's? She felt her whole world was crumbling once again, she felt stifled, she needed to sit down with a cup of coffee, to regain her sanity. With this, Natalie came over and announced, "Jannie's wedding will bring a lot of business to our store, she is such a high-profile lady, she knows so many people. It was her late husband that everyone knew, he was a successful businessman. Jannie was a background person, but when he died she stepped up, and now is the success story. Mason is just the icing on the cake for her, she deserves him, they make a lovely couple." Isobella couldn't help herself: "How has Mason contributed to Jannie's life? He seems much younger than her." "He was quite the party animal, but since meeting Jannie he has become a tamed pussycat, everyone loves him, and you can see why," replied Natalie. He is far from a tamed pussycat, I can vouch for that, thought a jealous Isobella.

That night at home while sipping a red wine, Isobella went over the day's events. Much of it she wished would just go away, but Lillian, that was a shock, plain Lillian, to think that she and James would be at the high-profile wedding, and she would not. Why did James always spoil things for her? As if their parents' estate saga wasn't enough, now this. Have another wine, Isobella, she told herself, it might help drown all your sorrows. With Conrad away she missed him terribly, everyone loved him, but she wanted him most, along with all his possessions. She went to pour another wine but the bottle was empty. The only thing left to do was to go bed and cuddle into Conrad's pillow.

The new fashions had arrived at the Guccia store and

the staff were busy hanging them in their appropriate settings, so each one could be displayed to its full potential. It was important to have them catch the client's eye as they entered the store. Isobella was asked to dress the window, as she had a good eye for detail. Just as the store closed, Natalie called a meeting with her staff. "I have decided to hold a cocktail party at our store and invite my good clients and their partners; this will be held on Friday after work. I have selected you, Isobella, to model clothes for the mature women, and Samantha for the younger set. I have spoken with Jannie McIntyre and she wants to bring some of her friends along who are looking for something special for her wedding. Now that we have this new shipment in we are able to offer some beautiful fashions. Please make yourselves available for the Friday night. We stand to make a lot of money from these clients, so let us excel at what we do best. There will be a bonus for everyone if we have a profitable night." Isobella loved the word bonus, so did Natalie, as she knew it would all come back to her store.

The day before the cocktail party, a tall willowy lady came into the store asking for Natalie. As Isobella studied her she had a vague recollection that she had met her before, but she could not think where. Their eyes locked, and suddenly the memory of her came flooding back. She was the lady at the mansion dancing in a flimsy gown with a martini in her hand. The one that took off in her car, the black Ferrari, when she gatecrashed their romantic evening. Isobella wondered if she remembered her, how embarrassing for both women, but it was a secret they both shared.

Isobella asked Natalie who the lady was. "That is my sister-in-law, Laura, she is my husband's sister. I'm not very fond of her. She is married to the CEO of Ferrari. She is not a regular client of mine, but she is a friend of Jannie's and is extremely rich. Laura and Michael, her husband, are invited to the cocktail party. We will pick the most expensive dress, and I'll get you to model it, Isobella, you will do it justice and hopefully Laura will buy it, it won't even make a dent in her bank account. There will be plenty of competition among the ladies, they will try to outdo each other, but that will be good for business," said Natalie, who was a shrewd business lady; she knew what to do and how to do it, this was her success story.

Natalie's sister-in-law Laura kept bugging Isobella. For goodness' sake, she was a friend of Jannie and she was sleeping with her partner. This was the pot calling the kettle black! She then began to wonder what Laura's husband was like, the CEO of Ferrari, that was some powerful man. Never mind, he would be at the party and she would meet him there. Perhaps a nice Ferrari was in line for Isobella; her mind was working overtime. If Laura could sleep with her Conrad, then she would test the ground with Laura's husband. This is what Isobella excelled at, revenge, especially if there was wealth attached.

Friday had finally arrived. Everyone at Guccia had their separate duties to perform at the cocktail party. It was to work like a well-oiled machine, that was Natalie's instructions. The fashions were displayed where they could be viewed by all who were attending. Natalie had a special surprise for Isobella. "You have brought a lot of business my way since starting here, I want you to choose a dress, any dress, and wear it tonight, and after the party it is yours to keep." Isobella was thrilled as she already had her eye on one of the new arrivals, it was beautiful, and would look exquisite on her, she had the figure to carry it off.

This will catch the eye of the CEO of Ferrari, this was her target for tonight. Laura wouldn't be able to hold a candle to her, even if she bought the most expensive fashion item, she was just not in Isobella's league. She lacked the sexy image that Isobella portrayed.

As the guests started arriving, Natalie was there to greet them all, she was the perfect hostess. Everyone was given a glass of bubbly, and told to enjoy themselves. When the store was full she announced, "Please feel free to walk around and view the fashions, we have Isobella and Samantha here to model any item you wish to see, enjoy your night. There is plenty of champagne." Most of the clients seemed to know each other as they all mixed and talked while viewing the fashions. Then there was excitement as the blood-red Lamborghini parked at the store entrance. Out climbed Conrad and he went around and helped Jannie. There was silence as they entered the store, then everybody cheered, it was as if a Hollywood A-list couple had gatecrashed the party. There was plenty of buzz after their arrival, they were the centre of attention. Isobella's jealousy was surfacing, but she had to keep it under tight control tonight; it should be her on Conrad's arm, not Jannie.

Then she spotted a familiar face with Jannie, it was Lillian, but of course they were old school friends. She wondered if James was here, as she had not seen him at this point. As she was glancing around she spotted Laura with a man, this must be the CEO. She edged closer to view Laura's husband. He was quite an upstanding gentleman, older than Conrad but nowhere near as handsome. His clothes were immaculate; yes, he was passable, thought Isobella, and he was very rich, this was definitely a target.

Isobella was drawing glances from all around the store, mainly from the male sector. The wives were too engrossed in the fashion scene to be noticing their men-folk. Then her eyes locked with Conrad's, her heart skipped a beat, as it always did when she saw him, she wanted to be in his arms, but he broke the gaze and walked over to be with Jannie. This hurt Isobella right down to the very core of her heart, it was as if she meant nothing to him. Right, she said to herself, the game is on.

She made her way over near the CEO of Ferrari and stood upright making herself noticeable. He glanced over at her and smiled, then he made his way over to where she was standing. "Are you here tonight to engage in buying?" he asked. "No, I work here for Natalie, I model the clothes that the clients want to see before they buy," answered Isobella. "You certainly have the figure for modelling, you look stunning, you captured my attention. By the way, my name is Michael," he said with a firm handshake. "Thank you, I will take your compliment to heart and keep it there," she replied as she walked away. That will make him think.

Isobella saw Lillian talking to Laura so she went over to her. "Hello, Lillian, nice to see you, have you seen any-thing you like? I saw you come in last week but I was dress-ing the window." With that she looked at Laura.

"Oh, this is my friend Laura, this is Isobella," said Lil-lian as she introduced them. "Hi, how are you? We have met before but we weren't formally introduced, nice to meet you again," replied Isobella with a smile. Suddenly Laura remembered where they had met. With that, Isobella had to leave as Natalie called her to model some clothes.

All the clients sat down as Isobella came out on to the catwalk; she carried herself gracefully, and the clothes looked beautiful on her. Natalie was so proud of her new recruit. Little did she know what lurked in the mind of her precious find. Isobella received accolades from everyone, but one person in particular could not take his eyes off her, and sadly it was not Conrad. The ladies were filling the dressing rooms, trying on their favourite pieces, ones that they just had to have. What with Jannie's wedding coming up, everyone wanted to look a million dollars.

Isobella was busying herself making sure that everyone was attended to, when she felt a presence behind her, followed by a hand touching her bottom. She swung around and there was Michael. "I think there was a hint in your earlier remark, am I right?" he asked. "Oh, I was just being polite," she replied, hoping that the seed was planted, and obviously it was. "Are you enjoying yourself? It is lovely of Natalie to put this party on for her clients, she has a good business head," said Isobella.

Michael thought to himself, she certainly knew what she was doing hiring such a 'hottie' to sell her clothes, that was a cunning business move. "Yes, I am very happy I came tonight, otherwise our paths would not have crossed. I would love to meet you out of work time," he commented, then he slipped her his business card. "Call me."

At the end of the evening no one walked out empty-handed, everyone was happy. Even Lillian had a parcel, but Isobella didn't see what she had bought. As Laura and Michael were leaving, she was carrying several parcels. She smiled sweetly at them and received a wink from Michael and just a blank stare from Laura. Isobella and Laura were enemies, as both had similar secrets to hide. Jannie and Conrad stayed behind for a nightcap with Natalie. "Come and join us, Isobella," called her boss, but she declined saying that she would get everything organised for the store to open in the morning. "I've got a good one in Isobella," said Natalie. "Actually, I have met her on several occasions, and still can't work her out," replied Jannie. Conrad intervened: "She can certainly sell the clothes, everyone seemed to like her. I noticed her talking to Lillian, I wonder how they know each other," he said. Then it was time for final farewells, and the store door closed.

"Well, Isobella, we have had a very successful night. You were a star, thank you," praised Natalie.

"I really enjoyed myself, it is fun when there are so many clients vying for clothes, tonight was magical," answered Isobella.

The next morning it was business as usual. New fashions were hung where last night's stock sold out. There had been a huge empty-out, so replacements were needed. When the store was empty of clients, Natalie called everyone into her office and gave them all an envelope. "As promised, here are your rewards. Last night was sensational, the turnover exceeded more than I could have imagined, so thank you all." She called Isobella aside and asked her not to disclose the amount that was given to her.

Meanwhile Lillian couldn't wait to tell James that she had met Isobella that evening and that she was employed at the Guccia store. She went on to say that she and Laura were in conversation when Isobella came and interrupted. "I introduced Laura to her, and they seemed to know each other, but there was an awkward silence between the two of them. It was the weirdest thing. Laura couldn't wait to excuse herself after Isobella said they had met but had not been formally introduced. I wonder what that was all about."

At last it was Sunday, now it was time to chill out. Isobella was waiting on a phone call from Conrad, she knew he was back from his business trip, because he had attended the cocktail party. Why hadn't he called her? She went to her handbag and took out the envelope that Natalie had given her, it was full of notes, and caught up in the envelope was the business card she had stuffed in, from Michael. She was livid that Conrad had not called, and still she didn't have his phone number. Now that she knew Jannie's surname, 'McIntyre', she looked her number up in the phone book, and rang.

"Hello, this is Mason speaking," said the voice. "Hi, Conrad, I have been waiting for your phone call. I need to see you, come around tomorrow," pleaded Isobella. "No, I can't as I am taking Jannie to an art show in the city, then we are visiting friends," he said curtly. "I will come on Tuesday night." Isobella could sense a feeling of rejection in his voice. She felt hurt once again. Should she make him pay, or move on? If she told Natalie the truth then she would lose her job, and this was her only contact with the wealthy jet-setters. She would wait until Tuesday before making a decision.

It was now Tuesday night and Isobella heard the Lamborghini pull up outside her home. She had gone the extra mile to look exquisite for him, and as she heard him kick off his cowboy boots at the door, her heart melted. She opened the door and threw herself into his arms. He closed the door but did not sweep her up and rush her to the bedroom; those days were past as far as Conrad was concerned, worry had taken over.

He wanted to tell her they were finished but how

would she react. He could not risk her going to Jannie so near to their wedding day. "I've missed you so much, Conrad, I could hardly control myself at the cocktail party. I wished it was me there with you and not Jannie, you and I belong together, please take me to bed, I'll prove it to you," sobbed Isobella. How could he get out of this, were the consequences too great, was he better to just play along? He took her to bed but his feelings were clouded by worry, it was over. As much as he tried to live the charade, he felt sick, this wasn't what an affair was about; he was frightened, this had never happened to him before. He couldn't even pay her out, as he had no access to any money, it was all Jannie's.

"I'm sorry, Isobella, but this is the end, I will not be coming here any more. I am marrying Jannie soon, she is the one I want to be with, you will just have to move on," said Conrad. "You're sorry, what about me? We had an agreement you and me, nothing has changed, we can still be lovers after you're married. I love you," she said. "No, Isobella, you fell in love with the mansion and the Lamborghini. I see it in your eyes — when we drive in the car you are happy because all you want is attention, you love the limelight, you are a superficial person, that is not what I want. Please don't call me at the mansion, don't contact me ever again." With this, he dressed and left.

Poor Isobella, her heart was broken. She had never been on this side of the fence before, as she was always the one that disposed of her lovers. Now the tables had turned. She couldn't go to Jannie and expose Conrad, as this would result in her losing her job. She would just have to move on. But for the first time in her life she actually found someone she loved, and now that was over, she had lost him. Just as well she loved her job or he would not have got off so lightly; she would just have to let revenge slip by this time.

She would move on once again, as there was another suitor waiting in the wings, and he was super-rich. She would handle this as a business deal, there would be no feelings attached.

Today the store was busy, clients were coming and going and Isobella was modelling clothes for potential buyers. As she glanced up she saw Michael entering the store. Natalie went over to help him. "I'm looking for something for Laura for her birthday. Can Isobella model for me if I pick out a couple of dresses?" he inquired. "Certainly, come here, Isobella, Michael wants you to model for him. I will leave him in your capable hands," said Natalie, and off she went. He picked out three dresses for her to model; Isobella did her job on the catwalk, with a little added cheekiness. Now was the time to tempt him, she thought, I have his undivided attention. Michael could not get enough of her, he was smitten. He chose the dress he thought looked sexiest on Isobella; never mind Laura, she wouldn't do justice to any of them. He walked over to Natalie and told her which one he wanted and asked her to wrap it up for him. He then approached Isobella and slipped her a note and a wink. She slipped it down inside her bra, it could wait till later. When he left, Isobella ask Natalie, "Is that Laura's husband?" "Yes, Michael is the big boss of Ferrari, he is a very wealthy man, loves his cars more than his wife." This was music to her ears: here was someone who put material things before feelings. Just the type of guy she was looking for, there would be no repercussions with this one. Perhaps a Ferrari was about to replace the blood-red Lamborghini.

That night as Isobella was getting undressed, the note

from Michael fell on the floor. She picked it up and sat down on her bed to read it. 'Isobella, meet me on Thursday night at 7.30 at the Plaza Hotel on Buckingham Street, I will be seated in the cocktail lounge. Michael' This was a very businesslike invitation, she thought, but that was all it was going to be, a business arrangement.

Thursday night came, and a beautiful-looking Isobella walked into the Plaza cocktail lounge. It was full of businessmen and they all focused on her as she made her way to the bar. This was definitely a male hideout, she thought. With that she felt an arm around her waist and it was Michael. He led her over to a secluded area.

"Cocktail?" he asked. "You look an absolute picture, I am the envy of all the males here." He then went to order drinks to be brought to their table. He came back with a parcel for her; it was in the same wrapper that Natalie had given him. "I want you to have this, Isobella, you looked so lovely in it when you modelled for me. Your image has never left me," he said quite passionately. "Thank you, Michael, this is unnecessary. What about Laura? I thought it was a birthday present." "What else was I to say to Natalie? I wanted to see you again on the catwalk modelling just for me, I had to do it to satisfy my own ends, I am really taken with you, Isobella. You remind me of the beautiful Ferrari I have sitting in the showroom on display," Michael replied. Isobella was delighted to be likened to a beautiful Ferrari, especially if it was on show.

After a couple of cocktails, Michael reserved a table for two for dinner; he asked for a table by the window so they could look out over the city lights. It was a rather romantic setting, thought Isobella. If only it was Conrad sitting opposite her and it was his eyes she was gazing into, but she had to bring her mind back to the present, that was the past. They chatted and ate a very expensive dinner, everything was of the best. He certainly oozed money, this is my type of guy, thought Isobella. Besides, she had an axe to grind with Laura: if she could bed my guy, then it was 'tit for tat'.

Michael walked her out to her car. He asked if they could do the same next Thursday. Then he took her in his arms and almost devoured her. That was most unexpected, especially from a man whose material objects came first. Isobella straightened herself up as Michael walked to his car. She would wait and see what he was driving. Out from the parking lot came a beautiful canary-yellow Ferrari with the emblem of a prancing horse gleaming in the streetlight. Suddenly the dreams of a blood-red Lamborghini were replaced with dreams of a canary-yellow Ferrari. And the dreams of Conrad were now dreams of Michael. Conrad never splashed money like Michael, but by now Isobella had finally realised he didn't have access to any money.

Isobella was so grateful that Natalie had given her such a cruisy job, one that she loved. She felt she had found her place in society, a place where she belonged, among the rich and famous, the beautiful people with beautiful clothes. This was definitely her world. If only Matilda could see her now, how proud she would be of her favourite daughter. It was only at times like this that Isobella remembered Matilda, when she needed a little spur of self-praise.

Conrad was not thought of so much, now that Isobella realised his station in life was that of a kept man. How could he keep her in the lifestyle she was accustomed to.

The big wedding was getting closer and the store was flat out with last-minute purchases. Everyone seemed to be invited, everybody except Isobella; even James and Lillian were going. She couldn't even have a peek at the groom, as it was in their private garden. Perhaps he was sleeping away from the mansion for the night before the wedding; she might get a glimpse of him in the morning as he was driving into the driveway to the mansion. She would park in the reserve carpark at the end of Lauderdale Street on the day, just in case.

It was Thursday again, how fast the week had passed thought, Isobella, as she parked her car in the Plaza Hotel carpark. The canary-yellow Ferrari was already parked up. She made her way into the foyer and through to the cocktail bar, wearing the new dress that Michael had bought for her. He would not be surprised because he had already seen it on her as she modelled it in the store for him. She could see that Michael was in deep conversation with another businessman, so she went and sat at the same place they sat last Thursday. Within seconds several men all made a beeline to where Isobella was sitting. Michael's friend at the bar tapped him on the shoulder: "Have a look at that classy bit of talent that has just arrived, she is stunning." With that he turned around and saw Isobella being hassled by other suitors. He strode over and asked them to leave saying he was with this lady. He apologised to Isobella, as he had not seen her come in. "I will be back in a moment, I am just tying up a business deal. I'll bring us a drink," said Michael. As he walked back to the bar his friend could not believe that Michael was with her. "Where did you find that gorgeous piece?" he asked. "She is a friend of a friend of mine. Her name is Isobella and she models fashions at the Guccia store on Fifth Avenue. Isn't she a treasure?" Michael said proudly. "You lucky man, I wish I had seen her first," he commented. They sealed the deal and said their goodbyes.

As Michael took a drink back to Isobella, he asked her to stand so he could have another glance of her in that beautiful dress. "You look stunning, you are some special lady," he stated. There were eyes everywhere peering at her, and Michael felt proud and very happy. He had plenty of admirers but being the full-on businessman that he was, he hadn't had time to think outside of his company. Even Laura took a back seat with him. But this was different! Around the racing circuits there were plenty of flash young ladies, but to meet someone so beautiful around his vintage was definitely an advantage. She would be more mature and not so petty as the younger generation. Little did Michael know what lurked below the surface with Isobella. His wife, Laura, was her own person; she had her friends and did her own thing, they had grown apart and had nothing in common any more. He supplied Laura with a generous income so she came and went as she pleased. Even to his friend's husband's bed.

Now he had Isobella, nothing else mattered very much, as he was totally smitten by her; he had been bitten by the love bug, never before had he wanted the company of a woman so much as he did her. Business had been his main priority but now that was changing. But to Isobella this was purely a business deal with no attachments. She was going to take all she could get with a thank you, and that would be followed by a goodbye.

Michael led Isobella into the restaurant and asked to be seated by the window, so they could again view the city lights. They drank expensive wine and dined on exquisite food, this was definitely a life she could put up with. Although Michael was very rich, he did not have the 'wow' factor; he was of average height, carried a little extra weight around his middle, and had a receding hairline. However, his style of dress was very businesslike, neat but predictable. Isobella had to put aside the comparison between the two men; one was very handsome but poor, the other was average but very rich. Really, there was no comparison for the lifestyle Isobella needed. Looks were important in the street, especially if one wanted to be noticed, and in bed, but other than that they didn't supply any material benefits. Wealth was the key to Isobella's heart; love was out on a limb for the time being.

As they were having a nightcap, Michael couldn't take his eyes of her, he just wanted to take her in his arms and feel her close to him. He asked to be excuse and left the room for a few minutes to talk to the reception person. "Do you have a suite available for tonight?" he asked. "Yes, we do, sir, it is the very best but expensive." "Expense is not a worry, please put it on my business card," instructed Michael, and he was given the key and told where the room was located.

Michael came back into the restaurant and asked Isobella to come with him. "I have taken the liberty to book a suite, please stay with me tonight," he pleaded. "I just want to have you to myself."

Isobella was surprised, although she had come prepared; she had slipped a lacy negligee into her rather large handbag just in case.

They went up in the lift to the 29th floor and walked along to room 119. When Michael opened the door, and entered, the suite was first class. Everything was of the best, this is what he wanted for Isobella. They walked over to the glass doors and looked out over the city; the views were breathtaking. Michael took Isobella in his arms and held her tightly, this was what he had wanted to do from the first moment her saw her tonight. He kissed her passionately, and wanted to move on, so tried to undo the zipper at the back of her dress but it would not budge. Michael was clumsy as he fought to get it undone, and he became a little frustrated. "You get undressed, Michael, I'll go to the bathroom and will be back in a moment," said Isobella kindly. She undressed and changed into her negligee. When she came out Michael was in bed, and he couldn't believe the vision that stood before him. He sat up and asked her to come to him. She slid into the bed and then it all happened, Michael's lust took over and it was like a business deal, all signed, sealed and delivered within a few minutes. Isobella had never experienced this before; it was obvious that he had not made love for quite some time, he was certainly not an experienced lover. No wonder Laura visited Conrad, as his bedtime manners were so different, he was considerate and loving and was the ultimate lover. Michael apologised and admitted he was excited, but promised it would be different next time. Isobella assured him that it was okay. It suited her, this was, after all, just a business deal, she told herself.

When she awoke in the morning a waiter had arrived with a breakfast trolley full of goodies. She could hear Michael singing in the shower, so she set up the breakfast for them. Minutes later he walked out as happy as a sand boy, smiling from ear to ear. He came and gave Isobella a kiss and thanked her for a wonderful night, but he was still apologetic about their quick lovemaking session. But Michael was the true essence of a businessman. Get the business over and seal the deal. Would Isobella be able to change his thinking in the love department? She could see that whatever he handled was all business to him, that was why he was the CEO of Ferrari. He was such an asset to the company, he was their 'kingpin'.

To Michael, business had always come before anything else, but something had happened since he set eyes on Isobella; now he wanted her to be with him. He couldn't seem to function properly, she was forever on his mind. Isobella had no idea where Michael lived, or for that matter she knew very little about his personal life. Only that he was Natalie's brother-in-law and was extremely rich, and that he had a wife that strayed. Oh, and he had a beautiful canary-yellow Ferrari. If this was all Isobella knew, it was enough to make her want to hang on in there. She could see benefits with Michael, if she played her cards right; all she had to do was straighten out his bedroom manoeuvres — with gain came a little pain.

It was now only three days to the big wedding. Jannie had come in several times for final bits and pieces. Even Laura was coming more frequently but she preferred to do her dealings with Natalie rather than with Isobella. These two rivals were very cautious, as neither wanted to spill the beans, so it was just as easy to avoid each other. One thing was for sure:their secrets were safe, for the moment at least. Isobella just presumed that Conrad and Laura's affair had finished. But this was not so, as Conrad could rely on Laura not to get possessive; it was a mutual agreement that suited both parties.

On the Friday night, the night before the wedding, Natalie decided to have a few drinks at work and invite her friends and good clients. This was sort of a pre-wedding night for Jannie; partners were invited. Isobella was asked to stay behind and help with the drinks; there was no store sales this time, it was purely social. It would give her a chance to see Conrad again.

People started arriving about 5.30 pm as the store had just closed. The first arrivals were Laura and Michael. Isobella hadn't given him a thought, only Conrad. When Michael spotted Isobella he made straight for her, and couldn't wait to tell her he that he was looking forward to their next night together. He even tried to touch her bottom, but she moved aside, as she didn't want Natalie to know about their friendship. Laura looked her way and stared daggers at Michael, but he dismissed her as if she didn't exist. Isobella decided it was time to move away from him, but he was always just one step behind her. Had Laura sensed something? This made Isobella feel uncomfortable. She wished Michael would just go away. The tables had turned, here was the hunter being hunted.

The room went silent as Jannie and Mason arrived, then everyone cheered and wished them well for tomorrow. He had to be the most handsome man in the room by far. Isobella's gaze slipped over to Laura who was standing there smiling at Mason, and she knew why and hated her for it. But then revenge was only one person away from Laura. As she looked up she saw Lillian and James talking to Jannie. Isobella panicked as she had not spoken with James since their mother had passed away. Then she saw them looking her way so she changed her position and moved behind the person in front of her.

James wondered how Jannie knew Isobella; there was only one way to find out and that was to ask. "Do you know Isobella?" he asked Jannie. "No, but she has been to the mansion several times, she even told me how my furniture was placed in my home, which I thought was strange, so I asked her to leave, although I find her quite pleasant in the store." It didn't take long for James and Lillian to work out why Isobella was hanging around the mansion, as they knew her past record with men. They could both see the attraction and hoped she had not overstepped the mark, but knowing her, the answer was most likely yes.

James and Lillian stayed at arm's length from Isobella. They did not want anyone to know they were related. They knew most people here including Laura and Michael. Lillian had gone to school with Laura and Jannie and they had remained friends throughout their adult years. When Isobella saw Michael talking to James she cringed, and hoped he didn't mention her name. She had to try to catch his eye and get him away as she was frightened he would let something slip. She caught his eye and smiled at him. That was enough for him to excuse himself from James and make a beeline for her. This did not go unnoticed by James, but how would Michael and Isobella know each other? Then the penny dropped: here was a very rich man with a prominent position, which would be reward enough to bring Isobella running into his arms. James felt sick; how many other friends did they have that she would have slept with? Her looks and figure were all she could offer men, but in most cases, that was all they required, nothing else mattered much. James hoped their paths would never cross again for a long time, in fact ever, as his feelings had not changed towards her. He had very few pleasant memories.

Now that Michael had Isobella on her own he pleaded with her: "Isobella, meet me tomorrow night at our same place." "I can't, Michael, you will be at Jannie's after the wedding do," she said. "I will leave at 8.00, please come, I have something special for you." "Okay, I'll be there, Michael," replied Isobella, and she walked away hoping no one else was listening. Everyone was enjoying themselves, especially the bride and groom to be. They were being congratulated by their friends and everyone was looking forward to tomorrow. Someone yelled out to Mason., "Where are you staying tonight? Are you up at the Plaza Hotel? We will call in later." "No, don't bother, I will be leaving here and having an early night to be ready for tomorrow," he answered. Isobella's ears pricked up when she heard this — so that's where he will be tonight. Ideas were floating around in her head; could she pay him one last visit before he became a married man, just one last time?

When everyone had left, Isobella helped Natalie to clean up and get everything in order for trading the next morning. Then she went home and changed into something fitting, something body-hugging, then drove to the Plaza Hotel. Just as she pulled up she noticed another car parking just ahead of her: it was a black Ferrari. She waited and out climbed Laura, all dressed up, carrying a bottle of champagne. Isobella wanted to get out and confront her, but as she shouldn't have been there herself, she waited until Laura disappeared into the hotel. The bitch, fancy visiting Mason on his last night as a free man, thought Isobella. But this was a laugh, as she was going to do the very same thing, it was just that Laura was first to arrive. She had been beaten.

Isobella was furious; she couldn't control her jealous streak, revenge was first and foremost on her mind. When the coast was clear she made her way over to Laura's black Ferrari and screwed off the dust cap and put a tiny pebble in it, then screwed it on again. This would put pressure on the valve and ultimately deflate the tyre. When she sneaked out of Mason's room and went to get in her car, hopefully the tyre would be flat, then she would have to find an alternate way home. Isobella then drove home, but the anger had not subsided. Why did he prefer Laura over her? She was much classier than Laura. She did not take kindly to being second best, she hated her rival even more after this, but one day, she thought, justice would prevail. But for who?

Today was Saturday, the sun was shining and it was a lovely warm day, just what Jannie and Mason would have ordered for their garden wedding. Isobella dressed in a classy pantsuit and drove to the public reserve at the end of Lauderdale Street. She parked where she was barely visible, to the oncoming traffic. She was here to get a glance of Mason. It will be interesting to see how Laura arrives, thought Isobella, she would probably have to get a ride with Michael, but then he was leaving early because he was meeting her at 8.00pm.

The wedding was at 1.30pm; it was now 12.30pm and cars were starting to wind their way down Lauderdale Street. Isobella didn't know who owned what car, but she knew enough to guess that many were very wealthy, because there were some pretty classy vehicles. She picked out James and Lillian's silver Jaguar and next came Michael's canary-yellow Ferrari. She strained to see if Laura was with him but she could only see Michael, but he was followed by a beautiful powder-blue Ferrari driven by guess who? Laura. Isobella was beside herself with rage; Mason last night and now this beautiful car, it was all she could take, so she decided to leave and go home and wallow in self-pity.

As she was driving back down Lauderdale Street she saw the Lamborghini coming towards her, so she pulled over and waved for Mason to stop. He pulled up opposite her, and the sight of his warm smiling eyes was enough to drive her into a frenzy, and she retaliated with anger.

"Why did you sleep with Laura last night? I wanted you, I came to the Plaza Hotel to be with you, but she was already there," sobbed Isobella. "why her and not me?" "I only wanted a casual affair, not a commitment, you were too possessive. You were a great lover but you wanted more, I didn't. Just let it go, Isobella, we are history," and with this he put his foot down and drove off to his wedding. Isobella sat and sobbed her heart out; it was over, he didn't want her, she didn't take rejection at all well, in fact she hated it. This brought on a worse state of revenge, and now it was Laura in the firing line. If only she stopped for a minute and realised that Mason ... Conrad was nothing less than a rat. He didn't deserve Jannie, as he was unfaithful to her behind her back, especially with her best friend Laura. But there are none so blind as those in love.

She pulled herself together and drove back to her home. She couldn't put out of her mind the happiness that was being celebrated at the mansion in Lauderdale Street. Especially Laura, as she was there with her lover, her husband and her powder-blue Ferrari; she had it all. Isobella made a promise to herself that this would all change for Laura; in the end she would be the loser.

The afternoon was slipping by slowly, until she realised she had an appointment with Michael at 8.00pm at the Plaza Hotel. She ran herself a bath and filled it with lavender bubbles so she could relax and try to regain her self-esteem. She felt deflated, this was not like her, but then she had never really been in love before. If love meant a broken heart, then this was a no-go zone for her. Little did she remember the hearts she had broken over the years, not love hearts, but innocent hearts of those people close to her.

Isobella knew that Michael was smitten with her, and

if she played her cards right, she could be one very lucky woman. Could she muster up a smidgen of feeling for him in her heart, or would Mason always be her 'guiding light'? She would take her time dressing, as tonight she wanted Michael to find her irresistible; she was on a crusade and that was to win his heart to get back at Laura. She put on a slinky pair of white pants, and a black top that would slip easily off her shoulders as to not cause Michael any embarrassment. She didn't want him to feel inadequate, as he was a powerful businessman. She felt he should be in control; this, Isobella didn't want to take away from him. She would slip into her pretty red negligee, in fact the one she had bought to match the blood-red Lamborghini. Was she still holding on to thoughts of Mason? Hopefully these would disappear when she gave herself to Michael. Tonight she hoped he was going to be a little more patient, and not treat it as just a business deal.

As she applied her last bit of make-up she noticed it was nearing 8 o'clock. She must finish and pick up her bag and head for her car. On reaching the Plaza Hotel carpark she could not see the canary-yellow Ferrari, so she parked and waited for a few minutes. There was no sign of Michael so Isobella decided to head into the cocktail bar and wait for him there. She went and sat in their usual place, and the waiter came over and asked her if he could bring her a drink. She ordered a cocktail.

Sitting at the bar was the gentleman that Michael was doing business with last week, so he told the barman he would take the drink to the lady. He walked over to Isobella with her drink and introduced himself, saying he was a friend of Michael, and he had seen her here last week. He took the liberty to sit down close to her, then she remembered seeing him at the bar. "How do you know Michael?"

she asked. "I do a lot of real-estate business with him, he is one of my best clients, he owns a lot of apartments all over town. Michael is the head man of Ferrari and is paid accordingly. We go back many years. He loves his cars and is a big fan of Formula One racing, in fact he is often seen around the circuits as a representative for his company. It is a pity his wife doesn't share his interest in car racing, as he is mostly on his own," he said.

This gave Isobella the lead she needed. She would ask Michael to take her to a car race, as she had seen them on TV and noticed the vibes and excitement surrounding the whole racing scene. She would love to experience this. "Hi, I'm sorry I am late. Hi, Toby, I see you two have met," Michael greeted them both. "You look lovely tonight as always, Isobella." Toby excused himself and left; if he thought he was in luck, it had just changed. "My car was hemmed in so I had to find the owner of the car in front so I could get out. The party was in full swing," explained Michael. "Are you sure you didn't want to stay, instead of being here with me?" asked Isobella. "I thought of you every moment I was there. No, this is where I want to be, here with you," he answered. "Tell me about the wedding, did Jannie look lovely, did you see Natalie?" "Yes, she was every bit the blushing bride, she looked radiant. I have a lot of time for her; she struggled, but she made it in the business world. I hope they will both be happy, she deserves it more than anybody. I hope the age difference isn't a worry as Mason is a handsome man," Michael replied. "Come, let us go to dinner, I am starving, I've been waiting all day for this."

They dined and chattered away about the day, both enjoying the atmosphere, then Isobella asked, "Michael, I would like to ask you something. I know you like cars, will you take me to a race circuit one day? I've seen it on TV and would like to be there in the flesh among all the hype and excitement." "Oh Isobella, yes I would love to take you. That is where I am happiest, cars were my life, that was until I met you. That was my surprise, I want to take you away for the weekend to Melbourne to the Formula One Grand Prix in two weeks' time. Do you think Natalie will give you the Friday off from the store? The company wants me to represent them on the circuit. We will fly out on the Friday morning," said Michael. "Please, Isobella, stay with me tonight and we will discuss this together."

With that they left the restaurant and caught the lift up to the 29th floor. Michael promised that he would not be so anxious this time and that things would be better. He put on some music and took her in his arms and guided her body close to his. He could feel the heat as he held her close, but he had to restrain himself and make this moment last. They stayed in each other's arms and danced together, until passion took over. Michael picked Isobella up and lay her on the bed and slowly undressed her. He then took his own clothes off and jumped onto the bed beside her; he just could not wait to take her as his, but he would try to be a little more patient this time. Isobella let him be masterful, as this would make him feel better about himself. She had to admit he had improved a little on his last performance. She felt a little pang of pity for Michael; he was a nice man, but it was quite obvious he had neglected his bedroom duties in favour of his work commitments.

Perhaps if Isobella hadn't met Mason, things might have been a lot different. She would play along and see where it went, and in the meantime Michael would spoil her. Had she found her prince at last?

They lay in bed in each other's arms most of the morning. Michael did not want to let go of Isobella. He would have to see her again before their flight to Melbourne in a fortnight. He was so happy to think that she would enjoy going to the racing circuits; if it worked out there would be plenty more flights around the globe together. His wife Laura was not the slightest bit interested in cars, only in her own jet-black Ferrari, and that was as far as her love went.

Sadly, Michael was a very lonely man with all the money in the world, but because he had put work first all his life, and achieved a top position at Ferrari, he suddenly realised that he had missed out on the finer things in life. He was treated to top service wherever he went, because that's what his company provided, but he had no one to share this luxury with. Now that Isobella had come into his life, things were going to be so much different. He could spoil her with gifts, as he certainly had the money to do so.

That afternoon after their goodbyes, Isobella drove home; she just wanted to relax and reflect on things. She went out into her garden and sat in her swing-seat, to rethink the past few days. Mason was lucky to have escaped her tangled web unscathed thus far, but would it come back to bite him in the future? Michael, on the other hand, was very kind and caring. Laura and Mason were lovers who both had wealthy partners, but that was not enough for either of them. And her life was just getting better, if only she could hold it together. She was happy, she loved her job working among the latest fashions and mixing with the elite, everything was going along nicely.

In the middle of the week Michael came into the Guccia store. He told Natalie that he was looking for something nice for Laura, and was Isobella available to model the items he chose.

"Isobella, would you please come over and model for Michael?" she asked. He winked at Isobella and took his time selecting several items. He just wanted to see her again. She was forever on his mind, and he had now realised that he was in love with her. He wanted to buy her some new clothes to take away with them next week when they flew to Melbourne. It wasn't that she didn't already have beautiful clothes but he just wanted to spoil her. She wore her clothes with such elegance and grace. He watched her modelling the clothes, and knew at that moment he was definitely in love with Isobella. As he left the shop with his parcels, Natalie passed a remark.

"All of a sudden Michael is taking an interest in Laura; he never used to come and buy her clothes. He is a good man, he has worked hard and deserves what he has achieved. He is a very wealthy man, a bit of a loner, but I suppose that goes with hard work and long hours." Isobella felt pride and shame at the same time, pride because of Michael and shame because of Laura.

Jannie had popped into the shop several times since her wedding, to talk to Natalie, telling her that she was really happy. Isobella was never far from earshot when she came in, as she was interested to know what was going on at the mansion, without having to quiz Natalie.

It was Thursday again, Michael and Isobella's weekly meeting. As she pulled up at the Plaza Hotel carpark, she noticed the blood-red Lamborghini parked at the back of the carpark, and not too far from it was the jet-black Ferrari. Could this be Mason and Laura? Surely they wouldn't be here tonight of all nights. Michael had not yet arrived, what would she do? She decided to go ahead and see if they were in the restaurant. As she passed she peeked in, and there sitting by the window were Laura and Mason having an intimate dinner.

Isobella was shocked, it wasn't even two weeks since his marriage to Jannie. She walked through to the cocktail bar and sat down in their seat. She didn't want Michael to see the two of them together, not for Laura's sake but for Jannie's. With that Michael arrived and gave her a kiss, then walked over and ordered a drink to be brought over to them. "I have some parcels for you in my car, I'll get them later," announced a happy Michael. They sat and talked, he loved every minute he spent with Isobella, she was so vibrant. "I am starving, let's go and have dinner." "No, Michael, let's just wait for a moment, I am not ready to eat at the moment, do you mind, we will order another drink," replied a worried Isobella. She wanted to let the other two finish their dinner and disappear before they went to eat. They talked about flying to Melbourne to the Grand Prix, with Isobella trying to fill in time. "I'll go and get us a table, I can't wait any longer," Michael said as he got up. "I am just going to go the ladies' room, you go ahead, I will see you in a minute," she answered. With that she left, hoping Laura and Mason were gone. Isobella went to the loo, then touched up her hair and applied some more lipstick. As she opened the door she could hear loud voices in the foyer so she had a peek and there were Michael, Mason and Laura deep in conversation. She retreated back behind the door and waited until the coast was clear, then made her way to the restaurant. Not wanting to let on she had heard or seen anything, she gave Michael a hug before she sat down; he loved it when Isobella showed him some warmth. They ordered their dinner and while they waited for it to arrive Michael was very quiet. Isobella asked, "Is something wrong? You are miles away." "I have just run into Laura and Mason coming out of here hand in hand. Can you believe it?" "Oh, Michael, I am so sorry," she said sympathetically. She did feel for him having to find out this way. "Poor Jannie, she doesn't deserve this, and to think Laura would do this to her best friend. Why couldn't it have been someone else? I thought Mason would have been happy being a kept man, but obviously not." Michael was angry, not for Laura, as their marriage was virtually over, but he did not want Jannie hurt, as she had been through enough heartache when her first husband passed away.

Isobella could see that he was hurting over this, so after they had eaten, she suggested that they both go to their own homes. Michael would not hear of this, it was now that he needed to take her in his arms and feel her close to him. They left the restaurant, then picked up the key and caught the lift up to the 29th floor. When they entered their suite, Michael went over and stood looking out the window, he was deep in thought. Isobella could sense that he needed to feel wanted so she went over and put her arms around him. Together they walked to the settee and sat down still wrapped in each other's arms. He could not remember how long it was since he felt this close to someone. This is what he wanted his life to be like, to sit at night and be able to feel the closeness of someone whom he loved.

Then he remembered the parcels he had for Isobella, so he excused himself and went down to his car. He came back with several parcels and kissed her before giving them to her. "I want you to have these, they looked fabulous on you when you modelled them, I couldn't choose so it was easier to buy them all. Here is another little package, this is special; please open it, I know you will love it," he pleaded. When Isobella opened it, there in a box was the most exquisite diamond bracelet which was glittering in the night light. She had never seen anything so beautiful. "Oh, Michael, what can I say? You have spent a lot of money on me, you don't have to do this, the bracelet is beautiful. Every time I wear it, you will be forever in my heart. I feel so spoilt," she said as she threw her arms around him. "Thank you so much!" Michael could not hold back any longer: "I love you, Isobella, I have been waiting to tell you this, I miss you when we are not together, the days seem long, I have never felt like this before, work has been my comfort zone but that is not enough any more. Don't say anything just now, I want you to have time to think about it." "Michael, are you sure this is how you feel, it is not because of what happened earlier tonight? You have been hurt, don't make sudden decisions, just take time to think about things," consoled Isobella. Michael was adamant in his reply. "Laura and I are over, and tonight sealed it. I am going to ask for a divorce, I can't live with her knowing what she has done to Jannie. She can do what she likes, but she is not breaking up friendships that have been in place for many years."

"Don't do this because of me, Michael, think about it for at least a couple of days." With this he put his arms around her and held her tightly, this is where he wanted to be, in Isobella's arms. They consoled each other, both having an axe to grind with what had happened earlier tonight, but Isobella's axe was unknown to Michael.

Isobella got up and went to have a shower only to find Michael right behind her. They both undressed and climbed into the shower together. The hot water poured over their bodies as he cuddled into her, and she felt the closeness between them thus leading to an intimate pleasure taking place. Michael was in heaven! They dried each other and walked to bed hand in hand, and snuggled between the sheets and fell asleep.

They woke up in the morning still in each other's arms. Michael had not been so happy for a long time. He was just realising what he had missed out on all these years, but now that he had Isobella, there would be plenty of good years ahead. Now it was time for them to part, Isobella thanked Michael for all her presents and told him he was a very generous man. They kissed each other goodbye and both went to their respective homes. There was some soul-searching to do on both sides.

Michael drove down his driveway to find Laura's black Ferrari parked at the door. When he entered their home she was curled up in a chair in tears.

"I'm sorry, Michael, that you saw us last night, I'm really sorry," she sobbed. "You have a week to pack your bags and leave. I can't believe that you would do that to Jannie, your best friend, that is betrayal. If it had been anyone else I could have overlooked it, but not Jannie. And so soon after her wedding day, that Mason is a scumbag, you deserve each other. I haven't made up my mind if I will tell Jannie as yet," said a furious Michael. "Please don't tell Jannie, don't kick me out, Michael, I want to stay," begged Laura. "No, you heard me, one week, not a day longer. You can tell your friends whatever you like. You can have one of the apartments until we sort out our affairs," and with this he went into his office and shut the door. That night he went to the spare bedroom, that is where he would sleep until Laura moved out, as he was disgusted with her.

Isobella was sad that Michael had found out this way about Laura and Mason, he didn't deserve this. Although she noticed that he wasn't too upset about Laura's betrayal, more about Jannie and how it would affect her. How could Mason be so stupid as to not keep faithful to his wedding vows for at least two weeks? Would Isobella have thought of this if Mason was still interested in her? She wondered what Michael would do, would he tell Jannie? She would not breathe a word to anyone, as no one knew about her and Michael. Just as well, or things could have been a lot different for her. Laura would want revenge.

Today was Friday and Isobella had managed to get the day off work. She was waiting for the taxi to take her to the airport, where Michael would be waiting for her. She had packed the clothes Michael had bought for her, she had the beautiful diamond bracelet on her wrist, and she looked a million dollars. As the taxi pulled up at the drop-off point, there he was. She had never seen him in anything other than a suit, but here he was in a lovely sports jacket and trousers. She had to admit this was a different look and she approved of it. He picked up her suitcase, and commented on how lovely she looked, and whipped her over to the check-in counter. Once all the flight details were confirmed, he led her up the stairs to the first-class lounge. Isobella had never flown first class before, so this was all new to her. Such luxury, all-day nibbles, and free alcohol, even showers and towels supplied, she was on cloud nine.

The flight went smoothly, they were fussed over by the flight attendants, and Michael was so attentive towards her. He was so happy his eyes never left her. When they arrived at the Melbourne airport and went through customs, he ordered a taxi to take them to their hotel, which was on the outskirts of the city near the race circuit. He had a meeting with his company at the circuit, so asked Isobella if she would like to come out to the race track with him. She agreed, so they freshened up at their hotel and then caught another taxi. When they arrived, they walked hand in hand to where the meeting was being held. They passed pit lane where all the Formula One cars were being worked on; only people with official passes were allowed anywhere near pit lane. Isobella loved the excitement and vibes that came from this area. It oozed wealth from all quarters, and the beautiful people all congregated around the young vibrant drivers, all vying for their attention. This was so much more exciting than the boring old art gallery; really, Conrad, what were you thinking? She noticed that everyone called out to Michael, they all seemed to know and respect him; this surprised her, but then he was a businessman as well as a gentleman.

Michael took her to the pit-crew café and ordered her a latte while he excused himself to attend his meeting. Isobella watched everyone buzzing around like bees round a honeypot. There was so much preparation in progress as the cars were being tested for tomorrow's Grand Prix. The mechanics were testing all the electronic equipment, it was nonstop maintenance. She loved the busy vibes that were surrounding her. It was the elite mixing with the elite.

Michael was back, and apologised for being away for so long as the meeting went longer than he anticipated, not that Isobella had noticed, as she was otherwise occupied with what was going on in pit lane. They caught a taxi back to the hotel so they could rest up before going to dinner with the company executives and their partners. They lay on the bed and both drifted off to sleep. Two hours had passed when Michael stirred, he woke Isobella as they had to change and go to dinner, as the others would be waiting on them.

Michael introduced Isobella to everybody. There were all nationalities, as they had come from all over the globe to attend this Melbourne Grand Prix. Everybody knew Michael, he seemed to be well known and well liked, this made her feel proud. Then she thought back to Laura, why did she not travel with Michael around these race circuits, and be among all this hype. The dinner was of the best, and so was the champagne that kept flowing, all paid for by the Ferrari management team, as they valued their top men. The hours slipped by quickly, next thing it was midnight, so everyone took leave and made their way back to their suites.

Today was the big Grand Prix day, and there was an air of excitement everywhere. The taxis were running behind time, as everyone wanted to get to the track. Michael had seats under cover in the Ferrari stand, so they could see the cars start from pit lane. It was a warm day, but showers were predicted for later in the afternoon, which would add to the excitement. Michael was in his element, as he was able to tell Isobella about the drivers and their teams, as he knew the 'who's who' of the car-racing world. She was a keen listener, and tried to take everything in, but there was so much to remember.

The race was about to begin in five minutes. The drivers all stood in a line as the Australian national anthem rang out over the circuit. They then made their way to their cars, and donned their fireproof head gear, their helmets and gloves. They did a lap of the circuit in their starting formation to warm up, then lined up on the grid waiting for the red lights to go out. Then it was all go, the race was on. Michael explained it all as it was unfolding, and that the red cars were their Ferraris. The crowds cheered and waved their flags for their favourites or their fellow countrymen. There were several crashes, as well as retirements for the cars that weren't performing. The hype built as the final laps were in sight, but now the rain that was forecast had arrived, which meant the cars had to go into pit lane and change to wet tyres. This was where the race could be won or lost, a quick tyre change was the game changer. Michael was really enjoying himself seeing Isobella caught up in the excitement with the rest of the crowds. First over the finish line was the opposition, with Ferrari taking out second and third positions. All teams wanted to come first but today Ferrari weren't quite good enough. Never mind — to have two drivers on the podium was great for the company. They waited to see the trophies presented to the drivers, who then sprayed each other with champagne. It was all over for another year in Melbourne, but in a fortnight Formula One would be at another circuit somewhere else around the globe.

That night back at the hotel, after all the race hype, they decided to dine in their suite with a celebrity bottle of champagne. They ordered room service to be delivered, as both were exhausted and just wanted to relax. After they had eaten and finished their bottle of wine they decided to settle for an early night. Isobella felt she wanted to show Michael how grateful she was, as she had been treated with total respect and love. She wished it was love and not just respect she could give back to him, but her 'ghost' was still lurking in the background; would he ever go away? She showed Michael the finer art to lovemaking; this he had never experienced before, it was all new to him. This totally cemented his love for Isobella.

With the weekend behind her, Isobella was now back

at the Guccia store doing what she loved best. She had such a wonderful weekend with Michael, she wanted to be able to tell Natalie, but this had to remain her and Michael's secret for the time being. Natalie did, however, have a piece of gossip for her: "Jannie called in and told me that Michael and Laura have decided to separate, and Laura is shifting into one of their apartments on Friday. I thought everything was fine between them, as he has been buying her new outfits, you know, Isobella, the ones you modelled for him." She had to busy herself for fear of Natalie seeing her turn scarlet. She was in shock, hearing this from her boss.

She had not discussed with Michael what his decision was on Laura, as she felt this was his business, and if he wanted to tell her, then that was fine. So now she knew that Michael must have told Laura to go, and only four people knew the reason why! To save face, Laura must have told friends that they had both agreed to separate. By saying this there was no blame on anyone. Laura's biggest fear was if Jannie found out the truth, and the only person who knew other than her and Mason was Michael. And, of course, Isobella, but no one knew she was a witness to that night at the Plaza Hotel.

A week had passed since their weekend away together and Michael was missing Isobella, but he had business to attend to at home. He and Laura had to sort out what was going and what was staying. Michael told her she could take their bed as he wanted no memories of her. Laura's apartment was on the other side of town, which meant he wouldn't see much of her, and she wouldn't interfere in his life. Isobella had no idea where he lived or what type of home he owned, as this had never been discussed. This is why Michael loved Isobella so much; material things didn't seem to matter. But was this a wrong assumption!

Once Laura had moved out and all her belongings were gone, Michael decided to pick Isobella up and bring her to his home for a night. He rang her to get her address, and made arrangements to pick her up on Friday after work. She wondered what part of town he lived in and what his home would be like. She had no idea.

She heard the Ferrari pull up at her gate so she picked up her overnight bag, locked the door, and walked out to the car. Michael was waiting for her, and he gave her a cuddle, then opened the door for her. They drove to a new part of town that she had never been before; there were new apartments and green areas, it was very upmarket. Michael drove down Parity Lane and turned into a driveway at the end of the lane. They stopped outside an ultra-modern building, built on three levels. "Here we are, Isobella, welcome to my home." He took her hand and led her up the stairs to the front lobby. As they walked through to the lounge area, there were glass doors opening onto a huge balcony that looked out over a stream that ran through the front of the property. It was in total contrast to the mansion in Lauderdale Street, but why this comparison? she asked herself; that was history, this was the present moment. Why couldn't she let go of the past? This was beautiful.

Michael's home was lovely, very modern with open plan living. There were many sculptures, and they suited this style of home. He had his favourite area that contained a large cabinet filled with all the Ferrari cars that had ever been made. As they had walked through into the dining room she noticed a portrait of a young boy on the wall. "Who is that, Michael?" she asked. "That is Mathew, our son. He is a lawyer in Shanghai." "Oh, I didn't know you had a family, you never talked about him," Isobella answered. "There are probably a lot of things you don't know, but you will have a chance to find out more about me," he replied. Michael explained about Laura moving out and taking a lot of their furniture, so that was why there were so many blank areas. They settled into a couple of deck chairs on the balcony and Michael opened a bottle of red wine. It was so peaceful watching the water meandering down the stream. "Michael, I would like to know a little about your life, please tell me," asked Isobella. "I don't want to bore you, just a quick version. I have two siblings, a brother and a sister who are both still alive. I went to university and did several degrees in commerce, which I passed with top grades. I then applied for an accounting position with the Ferrari company, where I was accepted. As the years went by I worked my way up the ladder to the CEO position, which I have held for ten years now. I met Laura through work, we married and had our son Mathew. I lived for my work, it was my whole life, apart from Mathew. Laura and I grew apart as she never wanted to accompany me to any work promotions, and when I was asked to attend the race circuits she showed no interest. I gave her a generous allowance, which allowed her to do as she chose, and of course she always drove the latest model Ferrari. She seemed happy with her life. That is the sum total of my life, and when I look back on it, it does not read as a fulfilling life, in fact it is quite empty. When I met you I realised what I had missed out on, suddenly work was not my whole life any more, you have now taken first place. You have given me a purpose away from work and that is what I needed. I love you, Isobella, and I would like you to think seriously about being part of my life, here in this home. Please think about it," said a heartfelt Michael.

The doorbell rang and Michael walked over and opened it. It was the delivery boy with the pizza he had ordered. He brought it through to the balcony table and they sat and ate it. "Now tell me about your life, Isobella," he asked. "Not now, but one day I will." She wouldn't know where to start with her life, as it was complicated. So much water had passed under the bridge, and plenty of dirty water at that. Michael would not be impressed with her past life, that was why it was better left untold. Especially when he knew her brother James — that was a worry on its own, as he would spill the beans on her.

As the sun went down, a chill came in the air, so they retired inside in the warmth. They put a movie on and cuddled up on the remaining settee. Isobella felt safe in Michael's arms, so why was it so hard for her to love him? Other women would give the world to be in her shoes. She told herself it would happen in time, but until that 'ghost' in her life disappeared, it would not be a happening thing. She felt for Michael, as he was a man as true as his word.

"Michael, can we wait and let the dust settle, let Laura settle in, before we make a decision?" asked Isobella. He agreed to wait, but not for too long, as he wanted her in his life full-time, forever.

The next morning they went shopping. Michael wanted her to pick a new bed that would be 'theirs'. As they walked around the bedding department, Isobella saw this beautiful four-poster bed, which immediately took her back to the mansion. She stood and pondered over it, but realised it would not suit Michael's modern apartment. "Do you like that four-poster bed?" he asked her. "Oh, I was just drawn to it, but let us look at more modern beds."

She could not get the four-poster out of her mind, as it was Jannie's; she even ended up in it on her own, as Mason could not perform that night, so he went to another room. They were not the best of memories. "If that's the bed you like, we will get it, it's not a worry," said Michael. No, it would be wrong for her to have that bed, as it would bring too many memories with it, ones she was trying to erase from her mind. She was frightened she would imagine herself making love to Mason, not Michael.

They continued bed searching until they found one they both liked and they lay on it to see if it was okay. It had a lovely carved headboard, so they made the decision to buy it. Isobella then went and chose linen and a beautiful duvet cover, covered in red roses. They had to buy a dining table and chairs, a cocktail cabinet and two La-Z-Boy chairs for the lounge. Michael wrote a cheque for the lot, and asked for it to be delivered later in the afternoon.

He drove Isobella back to her home after lunch, so he could be back when the furniture arrived. They made arrangements for next weekend, as Michael was away for the week on company business.

The Guccia store was very busy, and Isobella was still modelling clothes for clients. Midweek a lady came into the store looking for something a 'little special', as she put it, and she was accompanied by a man, presumably her partner. Isobella looked at him and recognised him as the businessman that Michael was doing business with at the Plaza cocktail bar. He was the one that brought her cocktail over and then seated himself very close to her. He was extremely good looking, but sleazy. She remembered he was a real-estate agent and his name was Toby. When his partner chose an outfit, he asked Isobella to model it for them. She felt quite uncomfortable as he winked at her;

she knew he was just there to perve. When they left the store she asked Natalie if they were clients of hers, but she couldn't remember them ever coming into her store in the past.

Later that day Laura came in to talk to Natalie, seeing she was her sister-in-law, just to let her know that she and Michael had separated. "I thought everything was fine with you and Michael, especially with him buying you all those lovely clothes lately," said Natalie. Laura looked at Natalie puzzled. "What clothes? Michael hasn't bought me clothes for many years," replied a shocked Laura. With that, Natalie realised she had overstepped the mark. She would never have believed that he would have a bit on the side, not Michael. "Oh, I'm sorry, Laura, I just presumed they were for you." "No, they were not for me, I would have thought he didn't have time for another woman, he hardly ever had time for me in his life." She couldn't wait to leave the store as the tears rolled down her cheeks. She said goodbye to Natalie and left.

Isobella had heard all this conversation and felt uneasy, but Laura had brought it on herself. Natalie called to her, "Isobella, I know now why Laura and Michael have separated; he has a lover, those clothes he bought, the ones that you modelled for him, they weren't for Laura, they were for someone else, what a dark horse. I wonder who his new lady is." Isobella pretended not to have heard this conversation and carried on hanging up the new arrivals. She was angry at Natalie for having presumed it was Michael's fault; if only she knew the truth.

After all that was happening, it was easier for Isobella to delay moving in with Michael. She wanted all the gossip and dust to settle, before she became the topic of conversation. How would Natalie react if she knew Isobella was the new lover? Would she lose her job? Of course she would, as it would cause embarrassment for Natalie and her clients. No way did she want this to happen. She worried how this was all going to pan out for her.

# 10

# What Would Isobella's Future Bring?



Several months went by with no more drama. It was common knowledge now that Laura and Michael's separation was caused by Michael. What would Laura demand as a marriage settlement, this was the latest; she would be able to screw him for millions, seeing he was the one in the wrong. Michael had issued Laura with divorce papers, which she had no option but to sign, anything to save her bacon with Jannie. If Laura was exposed, she would be shunned by all, and would have to relocate to another town.

The divorce settlement was settled between Laura and Michael; it was fair, not what she would have liked but then she had no choice. No one would know the amount, as it was none of their business, they didn't know the true story. It still hurt Laura knowing that Michael was seeing someone else, but she played around with the wrong guy, her friend's husband, that was why this all happened, she was the loser!

Isobella never repeated any of the shop gossip to Michael, he didn't know that the majority of people were blaming him for their separation. He was a man of substance, a businessman who minded his own business. This was a quality Isobella liked in him, and why she had a lot of respect for him.

Natalie had arranged for her close friends to come to the store and help celebrate her 50th birthday. Jannie had told her that she hadn't seen much of Laura lately and she couldn't understand why. Natalie made sure that she invited Laura and Lillian because they were old school friends. She asked Isobella if she would come back to the store at 6 o'clock and help her with the drinks and finger food.

Isobella went home and ran a bath so she could have a quick soak just to feel relaxed for tonight. Before she realised, 6 o'clock had ticked by and she wasn't even dressed. She grabbed the nearest dress from her wardrobe and quickly put it on, applied her make-up and away she went. It was most unusual for her to be late. Most of Natalie's friends were deep in conversation when she arrived, they all knew each other so they all mixed well. Laura and Lillian arrived together and thank goodness Natalie was at the door to greet them and give them a glass of champagne and offer them nibbles. These were two women that Isobella wanted to dodge if it was possible. They met up with Jannie so the three friends sat and caught up on each other's news. Isobella watched Laura's reaction with Jannie and she noticed she was uncomfortable, and why shouldn't she be, having to be in the company of her lover's wife, her best friend.

Then a strange thing happened. Every time Isobella looked in Natalie's direction she was staring at her with a puzzled look. This bugged her; had she done something wrong? In the end she decided to approach Natalie and ask if she had offended her in some way, but all she said was, "Oh, I'm sorry; no, it's okay, I just had something on my mind." Of course she had something on her mind. That dress Isobella was wearing was one she had wrapped for Michael, one he had bought for Laura. Oh no, this couldn't be happening, she told herself. Was Isobella the secret lover? She looked at Laura, then at Isobella, and of course Isobella stood out over Laura. But she would not be Michael's type, he was a typical businessman, he was a nice man but not for Isobella. She had not asked Isobella about her love life, and she knew very little about her personal life. All she knew was she was an asset to the store, she loved her job and they got on really well together. That was all she needed to know.

But that particular dress that Isobella was wearing tonight, she remembered it, as she had thought of keeping it for herself but Michael had picked it out before she had time to put it away. It did look fabulous on Isobella. Now a little window of light was opening. Was Michael getting her to model the clothes that he wanted her to wear, in exchange for favours?

Poor Laura, but why did she leave without a fight? She had a lovely home, Michael was a good provider, she could come and go as she chose, she got a brand-new Ferrari each year, it didn't make sense. Laura wouldn't be interested in another man, so why leave Michael? Natalie's brain was working overtime; how was she going to approach Isobella and tell her what she thought she knew? How would this affect their working relationship? She had a lot of thinking to do.

Everyone was enjoying themselves, then Jannie stood up and proposed a birthday toast to Natalie. All the girls cheered and wished her a 'happy fiftieth'. "And I would like to make a toast to a 'lifelong friendship' to two wonderful friends who are here tonight, Laura and Lillian," and everyone cheered again. Natalie and Isobella both watched Laura as she fought to hold back tears; they both had different reasons to feel sorry for her. It wasn't long after this that Laura and Lillian left as Laura had a bad headache. Isobella had managed to dodge both these ladies tonight as they all had axes to grind with each other. Lillian because of what they had gone through with Matilda's estate, and the heartache Isobella had caused. In no way had her family forgiven her.

When everyone had gone and Natalie and Isobella were on their own, Natalie asked her to sit down as she had something to discuss with her. She couldn't wait until tomorrow, she had to have an answer tonight "Isobella, tell me the truth, are you and Michael lovers?" Isobella went into shock and didn't know how to answer. She had told so many lies in her life, but these had stopped since she met Michael. "What makes you think that?" she quizzed. "I'll lay it straight on the line. The dress you are wearing tonight is a giveaway. Michael bought that for Laura, I wrapped it for him, remember? I want the truth." "Yes, Michael and I are lovers," replied Isobella. "So it was you who broke up their marriage. Poor Laura, no wonder she is distraught," said Natalie. Isobella was totally blown away by these false accusations. Could she trust Natalie by telling her the truth about Laura? She was her employer, she was sure the secret would be safe with her, and she had to protect her job. "Natalie, there is something you should know, but it must never leave this store. Michael caught Laura and Mason together at the Plaza Hotel, it wasn't even a fortnight after his and Jannie's wedding. They are lovers. That is why Michael told Laura to go, as he was disgusted that she would betray her best friend. None of this is Michael's fault, he is the innocent party. And yes, we were lovers before the Laura and Mason episode. Michael was a lonely man who happened to fall in love with me, that is why he came to the store all those times, it was to see me. I'm sorry this has happened, Natalie, but I can't stop how a person feels. Now you know the truth."

Natalie was shocked, she couldn't speak until she had digested all this information. Instead of poor Laura it was now poor Jannie. "Oh my God, Jannie would be heartbroken if this was made public, she loves Mason so much. Fancy that scumbag, a kept man, cheating on her so soon after their wedding day. I can't believe he would do that, he is the most handsome man I have ever met, but then the old saying 'Looks are only skin deep' obviously applies here." Natalie was angry at herself for blaming Michael for all this, when in fact it was Laura who brought it all on herself. She had always had a soft spot for him as he was a self-made man. Although Laura was her sister-in-law, it made no difference to what she now thought of her. "To think Jannie made a toast to a lifelong friendship tonight to Laura and Lillian, no wonder Laura fought to hide her tears, she will have felt ashamed of herself. That must be why she left after the toast," said an upset Natalie. "Thank you for being truthful with me tonight, Isobella, this conversation will never be repeated. It is so sad for Jannie that Mason is getting away with this, but one day he will hang himself. In the meantime, we must let Jannie enjoy what time she has left with him."

Tonight, Isobella could go to bed knowing that Natalie knew about her and Michael, that finally the truth had come out, and there would be no more persecution of Michael, at least by Natalie. She hoped it would not affect her position at the store, but that was yet to be discussed. She wished she was in Michael's arms, as he was a good, honest man. Isobella was looking forward to seeing him tomorrow.

Michael picked up Isobella and drove to Parity Lane to his home. They embraced when they got out of the car, and he led her out to the balcony where he had opened a bottle of wine for them to enjoy. They sat down and caught up on what was happening in their lives. Isobella had to tell Michael what had transpired between Natalie and her, and that she knew they were lovers. This did not worry Michael, as he wanted Isobella to move in with him, and when that happened, everyone would know. He was just waiting for her to make the move. "Tomorrow is my birthday, I have booked us a table at the Plaza Hotel and our suite for the night. I hope that is fine with you, Isobella," said a jubilant Michael. "Oh Michael, why didn't you tell me it was your birthday, I would have bought you a present. Oh well, I will just have to spoil you in some other way," she replied with a cheeky smile.

Michael's home was looking lived in again, with the new furniture. He wanted Isobella to position things where she thought they suited best, as he considered it 'their' home. The only thing left for him to do was to convince Isobella to come and live with him, he adored her and loved it when she was around. In actual fact, Isobella was a changed person within herself. She didn't have anyone to do battle with, as she had found peace at last. Michael was a calming influence on her, and suddenly all the lies had stopped. She loved her job, she could buy any clothes she wanted, and her money worries had vanished. Had the lioness been tamed? Was this princess wicked no more?

It was Michael's birthday. Isobella woke and went to get out of bed and bring breakfast into him. He pulled her close to him and held her tight, he just wanted to lie with her in his arms. He could feel the body heat welling up between them, her soft skin against his manly body, this was a recipe for disaster. He yearned to take her, and he knew when this happened she was his completely. Isobella responded, whispering sweet nothings in his ear then nibbling his earlobe. This drove Michael into a frenzy and out of control. They romped around in the bed, until the bedcovers all came loose and tangled around them. They could certainly cause havoc, but this left them utterly exhausted. When they awoke it was mid-morning and time for them to make arrangements for the remainder of the day.

This was a new experience for Michael, he had not had these strong sexual desires for many years, so this was a little out of his comfort zone. But it seemed a natural process with Isobella. Here he was on his 58th birthday, wondering why this had never happened before. This brought home to him that he had lived a very naive life.

They showered, dressed and set about making brunch; they wouldn't need much to eat as they were dining out tonight. As they sat down to eat, the phone rang and it was Michael's son, Mathew. "Happy birthday, Father, what are you and Mother planning for today? I hope you have something special arranged." With this, he had to break the news that he and Laura were no longer together.

"Since when, why wasn't I told, what happened?" he demanded. "Your mother and I had grown apart, we had nothing in common, so we decided to take a permanent break from each other. It leaves us both free to find happiness with someone else if we so choose," explained Michael. Mathew was shocked to hear of his parents' parting. He just presumed they would always be together. He told his father he would ring back later, as he had to digest what he had just heard. Michael knew he would be upset, as being an only child he loved both his parents. But now he was 35 years old, he was an adult, he would be able to handle it in time.

They had just finished the dishes when the phone rang again. This time it was Laura. "Happy birthday, Michael, I thought it would be nice if we went out for dinner tonight together, to celebrate." "I'm sorry, Laura, but I have made other arrangements. Mathew rang and I told him we had parted, he didn't take it very well, could you please speak to him and put his mind at rest? I told him it was by mutual consent, so if you say the same, it might make it easier for him to accept. Thank you for the birthday wishes," then he hung up. Isobella felt sad for Mathew finding out about his parents' parting on his father's birthday. She would remind Michael to call Mathew tomorrow. As for Laura, was she trying to worm her way back into Michael's life? There was no pity felt there.

They both dressed to go out for dinner. Isobella looked ravishing and persuaded Michael to wear a nice sports jacket and trousers rather than one of his many suits. Before they left, Michael told Isobella he had put something on the table for her. She went out to have a look, and there was a diamond necklace to match the bracelet he had given her a few months back. She thanked him and sealed it with a kiss. He put the necklace around her neck and thanked her for a lovely day.

They decided to go into the Plaza cocktail bar and have a martini before dining. As they walked in, the first person Isobella saw at the bar was Toby, the sleazy real-estate agent. His eyes lit up when he saw her, and then he gave her the trademark wink. She went and sat down while Michael ordered the drinks. He stopped to talk to Toby. "I see you are still with that 'hottie'; when you are finished with her, let me know," he said. "There will be no show of that. Isobella is moving in with me, I love her," Michael let him know before he got any ideas. With that he picked up their drinks and went over and sat down with Isobella. They sat and sipped their drinks, fondly remembering their antics earlier that day. Michael was so happy for having met her, as she was funny and exciting and made him feel good about himself. Perhaps it was a confidence boost by the opposite sex that helped bring his hidden feelings to the fore. Sadly, Laura had long given up on him.

Hunger got the better of Michael so they made their way to the restaurant. The waitress showed them to their reserved table by the window. Michael pulled out the chair for Isobella to sit down.

"Fancy seeing you here, Michael," said a voice from the next table. He looked around and there were Jannie and Mason. They must have just arrived. "Are you two on your own? Why don't we make a foursome and dine together?" she suggested. Michael agreed, and asked the waitress to move the tables together. "Isobella, do you know Jannie and Mason?" asked Michael. "Yes, we have met at the store," replied Isobella. Oh my God, he was still the same handsome hunk that she had made love to many times, she would never forget as he was the best lover, both she and Laura had experienced that. "I see you have moved on Michael, nice to see you, Isobella, what brings you out tonight?" she asked. "We are celebrating Michael's birthday," replied Isobella. They ordered two bottles of champagne to be brought to the table. All the time Mason was avoiding eye contact with Isobella. He wasn't the smiley person she knew, perhaps the kept life wasn't suiting him. What about Laura, was she still on the scene!? Perhaps he was shit scared of Michael spilling the beans on him to Jannie, and to have to share a table for the night would be an excruciating experience, but he had no choice.

Jannie was a lovely bubbly person, everyone liked her. Michael had a lot of respect for her, and now that he knew what a scumbag Mason was, he would make him suffer tonight. Michael had no idea that Mason and Isobella knew each other; how would he react if he found out? Although she had had no contact since he and Jannie were married.

Mason's life had stalled, his playboy antics weren't possible any more. Since their marriage, Jannie had hired a new PR person to handle all the overseas business so she could spend more time at home with him. This meant his philandering life had come to an end. He had cut Laura adrift since they were caught by Michael, as he was frightened he would mention this to Jannie. Mason had missed his ravenous lovemaking with Isobella, she was a lioness in the bedroom, it was just her wanting a long-term commitment that frightened him off. Now sitting opposite her and seeing how loving Michael was towards her made him envious, as she still had the looks and appeal. When he compared Jannie with Isobella, they were total opposites. Jannie was the wealthy one and Isobella was the beauty, and now he was finding that all the wealth in the world was not making him happy. He needed sex and that was missing, if only he could have Isobella in his life again. If he had to choose between the two women now, how different things would be; he would choose Isobella, she was exciting, Jannie was boring. Could he make amends with Isobella? he wondered.

Michael stood up as he wanted to make an announcement. "Isobella, I love you so much, will you marry me?" he asked. She was taken by surprise, this was unexpected, tonight of all nights. She looked across at Mason and almost melted when their eyes locked, but he had his chance, and turned her down. "Yes, Michael, I will marry you," she said. Was this answer made in haste just to get revenge on Mason? "This calls for celebration, congratulations to you both. I hope you will be very happy," Jannie commented. She still hadn't figured Isobella out, but she was very popular in the store, and Natalie spoke well of her, so any reservations she had, she would dismiss. Mason, on the other hand, felt hurt; now he could experience what it was like to be rejected, thought Isobella. This was 'tit for tat'. Mason certainly brought the wickedness out in Isobella.

The dinner was a nightmare for Mason with his boring wife, his lioness ex-lover, and Michael, the one that caught him red-handed with his wife. Suddenly this 'pin-up' guy, the one that had it all, actually had nothing.

Isobella, Michael and Jannie were enjoying themselves, the champagne was going down well and the food was delicious. Mason only picked away at his dinner, but drank plenty, to try to drown his sorrows. This did not do him justice, he became quiet and moody. "Mason, what is wrong with you tonight? Enjoy yourself, we are meant to be celebrating. I hope you both will be as happy as Mason and me," said Jannie. Both Michael and Isobella knew why Mason wasn't enjoying tonight, but both for different reasons.

After they finished dinner, and Jannie and Mason decided to leave, Jannie gave Isobella a hug and wished her well, then Mason gave her a hug and whispered, 'Meet me.' This did not surprise Isobella as she could feel the spark was still there. But out of respect for Michael, this was never going to happen, she told herself.

Michael and Isobella helped each other to the lift, as the champagne had certainly taken its toll. They hadn't seen each other in this state before. Michael had trouble getting the key in the lock as it kept moving. Eventually they opened the door and made it to their bed where they both collapsed. They lay still for a while, then an amorous Michael decided he wanted to undress Isobella. He rolled over to her side of the bed, so he thought, and tried to find the buttons on her dress but as he was fumbling around, he fell out of bed. As he fell he grabbed hold of the bedclothes, and pulled Isobella off the bed with the rest of the bedcovers. They fumbled away but couldn't do justice to anything so gave up and drifted off to sleep. At some ungodly hour of the morning Michael woke and found Isobella on top of him, his head was spinning, he couldn't move so went back to sleep.

When they awoke in the morning they were surprised to find themselves on the carpet and not in the bed. They were caught up in the bedcovers both half naked, and feeling the worse for wear. They weren't sure what 'did or didn't' happen last night. Then they noticed the breakfast trolley parked up by their bed. How did that get there? The waiter must have brought it in and left it.

What would he have thought? he must have seen them lying on the carpet among all the bedding. When they recovered, and ate a little breakfast, they both burst out laughing. What an unforgettable night, they would never forget Michael's 58th birthday. Now to face the embarrassment when they went to pay their account.

The breakfast waiter had knocked at the door and there was no reply, so he checked his menu list, and yes, suite 119 had ordered breakfast. He unlocked the door and walked in to find two people half naked and tangled up in the bedclothes, lying on the carpet. He left the trolley and ran out of the room, hoping they didn't wake and see him. He caught the lift and ran to the kitchen and told everyone what he had just seen in room 119.

When Michael and Isobella arrived at reception there were a lot of staff hanging around in the foyer. Michael went to pay, and the reception person asked, "What suite number, sir?" Michael leaned over and very quietly said the room number. "Oh, suite 119, certainly, sir," repeated the reception person. This was the key word to the staff, so they all knew this was the couple that preferred the carpet to the bed, thus sending sniggers all around the lobby. Poor Michael and Isobella couldn't wait to get out of the hotel, and burst into laughter themselves.

They drove back to Parity Lane, both feeling the worse for wear. Michael vaguely remembered proposing to Isobella last night. Did she accept? He could not remember. He would have to ask her again. "I think I proposed last night; did you say yes?" he asked Isobella. She made out she didn't remember the proposal. "I don't remember." "Will you marry me, Isobella, please say yes," he pleaded.

"This is the second proposal I have had in twenty-four hours, I will accept this one," she answered with a smile. This was certainly a day to remember!

Later in the week Jannie ran into Laura at the PostShop and they arranged to meet for lunch. It was here Laura learnt that Michael had proposed to Isobella, and that she had accepted. This broke Laura's heart as she had hoped to return to him. She was at a loss since Michael asked her to leave, as he was her stable backstop. But why had he chosen Isobella? She was also Mason's lover. One day she would tell Michael this, but not at the moment because he had things he could tell Jannie about her. It was a no-win situation.

Michael and Isobella talked about their wedding. He wanted her to have what she wanted, if it was a flash wedding he would be happy. But Isobella could see obstacles in the way, namely James and Lillian; they would certainly let out some secrets that she wished to remain hidden in the cupboard. She decided to keep it low profile, in fact she suggested they go away together and get married then tell everyone. This suited Michael as he wanted her so badly, nothing else mattered. The only person to know would be Natalie as she would have to get time off work. They decided it would all happen in two weeks' time. Isobella would stay at her home until they went away together to be married. Natalie wanted her to stay on at the store after they came back, and Isobella agreed, as Michael would still be working. He was needed at his job, but it would no longer rule his life, as he had found a new interest.

A new shipment of fashions had arrived at the store, so the staff were busy setting up display areas. Isobella was dressing the window when she heard a tap on the glass. There standing outside the window was Mason, and he signalled for her to come out. Isobella said she was going out to check on her window display. She walked out the door and met Mason on the footpath. "I have missed you so much, Isobella, please come back into my life," he pleaded. She looked into his eyes and that glint was still there, and that nearly forgotten yearning had returned; she felt the warmth taking over her body, something that only happened with Mason. It was then she realised she still loved him, she wanted him desperately, but now was not the time. Isobella thought it was the blood-red Lamborghini and the mansion that was the attraction but these items were only disguising her love for Mason. She still found it hard calling him Mason as she loved him as Conrad. "Michael is a good man, I won't let him down, now is not the time," she replied.

"Just tell me you feel the same for me, Isobella, that's all I want to hear," he pleaded. With this she smiled, and walked back into the store. Mason's plea was left unanswered.

Isobella couldn't wait for the next week to go by. The meeting with Mason had thrown her off balance. She cared dearly for Michael, but she was still in love with Mason, he was the only man that had reached into her heart and messed with her heartbeat.

Isobella's mind was all over the place. After work she walked the streets, just to clear her head; she was going somewhere, but where it didn't matter. She kept walking, then she spotted a shabby little booth tucked away in a side alley. This took her attention away from everything else. What could this be? She looked up at the sign: 'Tilly Dunnage, Fortune Teller, come and have your future told'. Tilly Dunnage, Tilly Dunnage, what a sad name, thought Isobella as she kept repeating it to herself. Was she a convict child sent out from God knows where? Who would call a child that name, what hope would she have in life? No wonder she was tucked away in a back alley. As she carried on walking, the name kept ringing in her mind, and she found herself repeating it over and over. She just had to go back and see it again.

As she was standing there looking at the signage, a little old lady shuffled out of the booth. She was dressed in black and had a lace shawl over her head. The shawl fell down around her shoulders. She looked into Isobella's eyes for a moment, then said, "Come with me, I have your future in my crystal ball, you need to know there is sadness." Isobella felt she was waking from a dream; who was this forlorn little lady called Tilly Dunnage? She felt her hand being taken and she was being led into the tiny booth. There was barely enough room for two people and the table with the crystal ball. She asked Isobella to be seated, then she reached for her shawl and put it over her head and face. She closed her eyes and sat for a few minutes, then held her hands just above the crystal ball. She reached out and touched Isobella on the forehead, then took her hands and placed them palms up on the table. Isobella felt a cold shiver down her spine, then words started flowing from Tilly's mouth: "I see sadness, I see riches, there is a courtroom, in the background there is a man smiling. There is a figure haunting you, a figure from the past, there is something you really want but you can never have. Be careful, there is a traitor. Love comes and goes, you will never find what you are looking for," then Tilly reached out and touched Isobella's forehead again and added, "Beware, there is danger not too far away. I can feel it." With this, Tilly lifted the shawl from her face. Isobella could see a sad mystical look in her very dark eyes.

There was something about her, was it just her name or was it deeper? Isobella stood up and thanked her and left a $100 note on the table next to the crystal ball. As she left the tiny booth, Tilly shuffled out onto the footpath and watched Isobella disappear. "What beauty, but no heart," muttered Tilly to herself.

She sat on a park bench trying to make sense from her reading. Sadness, that must have been Matilda's passing; richness, that must be Matilda's estate; a courtroom, that must be the court case with James but he wasn't smiling; someone haunting her from the past, that must be Matilda; but the rest, it was all a mystery. Dear old Tilly must have been confused, she seemed to get Isobella's past mixed with her future. She took some comfort from this, knowing that so far, she had got many things right. But a traitor, who could that be, and danger, what did she mean by this?

Now there was the long walk back; she had to go past Tilly's booth again. This name would not leave her. As she got to the top of the street, she stopped and looked back and she thought she could see the outline of Tilly standing on the footpath waving to her. Was this just an image etched in her mind or was she actually standing there?

Only two more work days until Isobella and Michael were leaving on holiday. She was busy unpacking a box of accessories that had arrived at the store, when she heard Natalie calling her: "Isobella, there is a gentleman here, he wants you to model a couple of items for him." When she saw who it was, her heart sank; it was the sleazy real-estate agent Toby and he was on his own. He had picked out three items for her to model. He said he was looking for something special to surprise a lovely lady. Isobella changed and modelled the three dresses he had chosen.

His eyes were locked on her and she could feel him undressing her with every step she took. "Which one do you like best, Isobella?" Toby asked. "I need a bit of expert advice." She had a bad feeling about this guy right from the first time she set eyes on him. She didn't really want to help him with any advice, but it was part of her job. She left Natalie to wrap the chosen dress. When he left the store she asked Natalie if she knew anything about him.

"No, I don't have a clue, remember he came in with his partner one other time? I thought he was a friend of yours, as he asked for your address."

That night when Isobella got home there was a parcel on her doorstep. She unlocked her door and took the parcel inside and put it on the bench. She made herself a coffee and then unwrapped it. As she peeled the first layer off she could see it was from their store. When she saw the dress, it was one of the ones she had modelled earlier for the sleazy real-estate agent. She felt sick, as she had done nothing to encourage him, and to top it off, he was a friend of Michael. Should she tell him or just let it pass? As she cleared away the wrapping paper, she found a note saying, 'Isobella, you are one sexy lady. When Michael's finished with you, I will be waiting.' It was unsigned. She was angry and couldn't wait for her and Michael to be married, that would put an end to this sleazebag, she thought. She left the dress in the bag and shoved it away in a wardrobe. This would be one dress that would never be worn, she assured herself.

Today went by fast and Isobella was looking forward to her week off. Tonight she would pack everything she needed to go to Michael's and put it on the lounge floor so they could just pick it up as they were leaving. She had decided not to sell her home, she would keep it in the meantime.

This was her last night in her home. She ran a bath and put in some lavender crystals to make her feel sleepy. She soaked for almost an hour until she was totally relaxed. She put on her silk dressing gown, nothing else, as she was going to bed shortly. She curled up on the settee, and felt herself dozing off. She was suddenly woken by a loud knock on the door. Oh, it must be Michael, she thought, so went and unlocked the door. Standing there was a very inebriated Toby. As she went to shut the door he had his foot jammed in it, stopping it from closing. He pushed her back and shut the door behind him, and staggered towards her. "I see you are waiting for me, Isobella," he said. He lunged at her and grabbed her gown pulling it from her. There she stood stark naked. Toby's eyes feasted on her body, as she tried to digest what had just happened. He then came at her like a madman and in a split second she reached for the standard lamp and whacked him on the head. Down he went totally out to it, falling at Isobella's feet. She ran to her bedroom and put some clothes on. When she came back he was still out cold on the floor. She took some deep breaths to steady her nerves. What could she do? She bent over and saw blood coming from his head, so she rang for an ambulance to come straight away. When they arrived, she explained what had happened, and they wanted to know if she wanted to lay charges against him; if so, they would call the police. "No, I don't think he would have done this if he was sober," she answered. They loaded Toby onto the stretcher and carted him off to hospital.

Isobella sat on the settee and regained her composure. Then her mind went back to Tilly Dunnage; was this the danger she was warning her about, how would she know this was going to happen?

The next morning as Isobella woke, she was still feeling upset over what happened last night. She worried about what damage she had done to Toby. She rang the hospital to see if he was all right. She told the hospital that she was the person who rung for the ambulance, so they put her through to the ward he was in. The nurse that spoke with her said he was feeling very sorry for himself, he couldn't remember what had happened or where he was, in fact the night was a total blur, whether caused by the blow to the head or just an alcohol-induced memory loss. Either way he was very lucky. She decided not to tell Michael about this incident, as Toby would probably receive another blow to the head. Hopefully he had learnt his lesson. Isobella was pleased he couldn't recall anything about the night as she was spared the embarrassment of being seen in the nude by Toby.

When Toby woke from his drunken stupor his head was throbbing. He asked the hospital staff what had happened to him, how did he end up in hospital. They went to the notes and read what was written, and told him he had gone to a lady's home and tried to attack her, she was petrified so grabbed a lamp and hit him on the head. Then she had the decency to ring for an ambulance. He had no idea this had happened, and who was the lady. "It is written here as Isobella, she rang to see that she hadn't killed you. That is some forgiving lady. I think you owe her an apology, it must have been a terrible ordeal for her, especially at home on her own," reported the nurse.

When he heard Isobella's name he felt so ashamed, he just wanted to crawl under the blankets and never wake up. He was smitten by her and to think he attacked her in her own home. Michael was one of his wealthiest clients; what consequences would come out of this? Was he going to be sacked by the company? In the worst-case scenario he would certainly lose his dealings with Michael. This would be a huge blow for his company. He would just have to wait and see. "Excuse me, sir, your wife has just arrived to take you home. You will have some explaining to do to her. I will give you some painkillers, you will have to come back in a week so we can check on those stitches in your head," said the duty nurse. "Oh and don't forget, an apology to Isobella wouldn't go astray."

# 11

# A New Chapter in Isobella's Life

Today was the start of a new life for Isobella. She was now living with Michael, this was her new home. Parity Lane was a quiet cul-de-sac with new apartments lining each side of the lane. Most of the owners were middle-aged and retired couples who obviously had a bit of money behind them. Michael didn't know many of the couples as he was an unknown quantity to them and this is how he liked to live his life.

Today was the start of their week away together, and in this time, they were going to find their little church and get married. They put their suitcases in Michael's yellow Ferrari and headed off on a journey to find where they would take their nuptials. They had no idea where their little church would be, but when they saw it they would know. Isobella had packed a lovely dress for their special day.

Michael had several work-related calls to make as CEO of the company, and this was fine with Isobella, as she knew how important his work was to him. This was going to be a two-way partnership, with both sharing each other's work commitments.

They drove up the West Coast where they passed through quaint little fishing villages, stopping at each one and exploring what was on offer. Michael loved being with Isobella, and each day his love grew stronger.

He knew his love was deeper than Isobella's, but this did not matter to him, he was so happy. He was extremely rich, but never tried to buy her attention, although he loved giving her gifts. She was warm with Michael, touching him, holding his hand, and hugging him, as he was a good caring person.

On their second day, they started off early in the morning as Michael had a work call to make. When they arrived in the town he dropped Isobella off so she could browse the shops. Since her encounter with Tilly Dunnage she was drawn to the back streets to explore the alleyways. This was not like her, as the first places she made for were the upmarket shopping malls. Now she loved reading the signage on the outside of shops that were tucked away. She had not mentioned Tilly to anyone, not even Michael, this was her little world. But that encounter was still fresh in her mind, as if it were yesterday. She wondered why she kept repeating that name time and time again, and then to go back and read it again. But if she hadn't gone back their paths would never have crossed. Was this fate? she kept asking herself; did Tilly see things that she wanted to warn Isobella about? The danger warning, did this relate to Toby? she wondered. She couldn't see that any of the past happenings would have anything to do with the future. But was it Isobella that was confused, not Tilly? The reading was her future, nothing to do with her past, but she had matched it to her past. They hadn't happened yet, this she would discover. She did wonder who the traitor might be!

She met Michael for lunch and they decided on a little French café. They ordered pastries and lattes. After lunch they continued on their way, stopping at places of interest. That night they stayed at a country homestay, something neither had done before, so this was a new adventure for them. They drove down a long driveway which opened up to a lovely setting with a large chalet-type home. There were three cars parked in the driveway, so they pulled up beside them. As they climbed out of the car, they were greeted by a robust rosy-cheeked lady welcoming them to her homestay. She showed them to their room, which was clean and homely, and pointed to the end of the hallway, telling them there was a guest lounge for their use. A true country roast dinner was at 6.30.

After settling they went down to the lounge where they met another couple. They introduced themselves and started to converse with each other. The men's conversation centred around cars and the girls talked fashion. As it turned out, Suzie knew Natalie, and mentioned about Natalie's only child, a daughter, who had been killed in an accident. Isobella was surprised, as she didn't know about this, but then she and Natalie never discussed personal things, mainly work-related issues. They were interrupted by the dinner gong, so made their way to the dining room.

After a lovely home-cooked dinner, they went back to their room and sat together on the settee, as they were feeling quite tired.

"Time is running out, Isobella, we have to start looking

for our church, I am not returning home an unmarried man. We can't start our honeymoon until we are married," laughed Michael. "Tomorrow is the day." They both showered and climbed into bed exhausted, and dropped off to sleep.

Today was the day! They had breakfast, thanked their hosts and started on their journey, travelling further up the coast. At lunch time, they stopped at a little town by the sea, and had some lunch. As they were walking back to their car they saw a church steeple in the background, so made their way to where the steeple was. As they neared, there in among some huge established trees was a little stone church. They both knew the moment they saw it, this was their church, the search was over. Michael saw a lady in the church grounds and asked her if it was used for weddings. "We just had one yesterday, it was lovely," she said. "Do you know where I can find a marriage celebrant?" asked Michael. "Yes, one lives right next door, over there," she pointed. Michael went over and knocked on the door, and asked the lady if she was a marriage celebrant. Yes, she confirmed she was. He asked her if she would be available tomorrow morning at 11.30, as he wanted to get married. She was taken by surprise, but yes, that could be arranged. Michael said he would arrange flowers with a florist, but where could he get a photographer? "All taken care of, my husband usually does the photographs," said the celebrant. Now all Michael had to do was turn up tomorrow!

Michael went over to Isobella and told her she would be his wife tomorrow morning. They booked into a hotel for the night, then he went and found a florist. He asked for the church to be filled with flowers tomorrow morning at 10.30, and left his credit card as a guarantee. He requested a bouquet of red roses to be made, as he wanted to give them to Isobella to hold while they exchanged vows. He loved red roses, as he thought of them as the flowers of love. As he was leaving the shop he saw a box of dried rose petals, and asked if they could be sprinkled down the aisle, so Isobella could walk among them. He wanted her to be as happy as he was going to be.

Today was their wedding day. Michael ordered a taxi to pick Isobella up at 11.15, as he wanted to drive to the church and be waiting for his bride when she arrived. This gave her time to dress and surprise Michael. No one could have been happier than Michael, because at last Isobella was going to be his. It had nearly been a year since he had touched her bottom at the Guccia store party. He still didn't know why he had done that, because it was out of character for him, but she was like a magnet. From the first moment he saw her, he wanted her to belong to him.

As Michael walked into the little stone church, it had suddenly become alive; the flowers had given it life, they were beautiful, and the rose petals were scattered down the aisle putting a finishing touch to it. The bouquet of red roses was on the alter, waiting for Michael to give to Isobella.

The marriage celebrant had just arrived. She was a pleasant lady and asked Michael questions about himself and his bride, so she could add a personal touch to the ceremony. He checked to see if he had the most important item, the ring. He bought the best for her. It cost him a hefty packet, but she was worth every penny he had spent. He had never discussed his wealth with Isobella, but that would change when they became husband and wife.

Michael heard the taxi pull up outside the church. He waited for a few minutes, then turned around to see Iso bella walking towards him. She looked stunning in her cream Chantilly lace dress. Michael felt so proud, and in a few minutes, she would be his wife. It was at that moment when Isobella looked at Michael that she saw Bartholomew, her father. Was this why she liked him, not loved him? Was he a father figure? Had she now become Michael's little princess?

Michael reached for the bouquet of red roses and gave them to her, and took her hand in his. He was happy he didn't have to share her with anyone else today, only the celebrant, the photographer and himself. This was their moment in time. The celebrant started the ceremony, welcoming Michael and Isobella to this sacred place of prayer to exchange their wedding vows. The service was lovely, and when Michael put the wedding ring on her finger, she had never seen one so exquisite. Isobella had wanted to buy Michael a ring to exchange, but he wasn't into jewellery. Then the long-awaited words, "I now pronounce you husband and wife, you may kiss the bride". Michael took Isobella in his arms and kissed her, now she was his.

They walked to the back of the church and sat in the back pew, to savour the moment and the beautiful flowers that decorated 'their' little church. Together they made a vow to return each wedding anniversary, to this very place to celebrate. As they were leaving the church, Michael asked the celebrant if she would like to take the flowers to the local hospital. She accepted and thanked them for their kindness. With this they climbed into their car and drove off.

It was mid-afternoon and they were leaving the coastline to drive inland. They would just keep driving until they found somewhere romantic to stay the night. Isobella loved the way nothing fazed Michael, he accepted life as it happened, nothing had to be planned ahead. Perhaps because his work was so organised, when he was away from it he relaxed.

They didn't have to drive far inland before they spied little tree-top cabins built on stilts above the forest canopy. They looked so romantic perched up in the air.

At the entrance was a sign 'Hideaway Lodge' licensed restaurant, and tree-top cabins. That will do us, thought Michael, so he drove down the driveway. They pulled up at the reception area, and Michael went in to inquire if they had a honeymoon suite available for the night. Yes, they could do that, so he asked for a bottle of the best champagne to be delivered to their cabin once they settled in. The reception person took Michael to the cabin and up the steps and opened the door for him. It was perfect. The net curtains were blowing in the breeze, and the bed was a four-poster with a canopy. Just the bridal suite he would have ordered. At last Isobella could sleep in her four-poster bed, as his mind went back to the furniture store when she was standing admiring that same-style bed.

Michael drove up and parked in their allotted park. He went around and opened the door for his wife, then he looked at the steps. How was he going to carry her up there? "If I was twenty years younger I would have picked you up and run up the steps, but alas, not now," sighed Michael. They took each other's hand and climbed the steps together, then he picked her up and carried her across the threshold. Isobella loved the cabin; she walked over to the sliding doors and opened them, and all they could see was the blue sky and the green forest. They walked out onto the balcony, and Michael took Isobella in his arms. "I love you so much, you have made me very happy. What does it feel like to be Mrs Reynolds?"

To this Isobella replied, "You are a wonderful man, Michael, I don't deserve you." They stood in silence in each other's arms, and listened to the forest birds singing their praises. There was a knock on the door and the bottle of champagne had arrived. Michael popped the cork and filled two glasses of bubbly, then they toasted each other. "Here's to my beautiful wife and a happy life together."

A chill in the late-afternoon air brought them inside the cabin. It was only then that Isobella noticed the four-poster bed, and suddenly the 'wanted to be forgotten memories' came flooding back. Today of all days. She hadn't given Mason a thought in the past few days. Now he was here with her and Michael. They sat together and talked about their day, both delighted they had found 'their' little church. Isobella thanked Michael for arranging the beautiful flowers and her bouquet of roses. "Isobella, I have a little something for you," and Michael handed her an envelope. Inside the envelope was a set of car keys. "What are these for, Michael?" she asked. "It is my wedding present to you, you will just have to wait till we get home," he said. She had no idea what he had bought her. "You are so kind, Michael, you have been a good influence on me, you have definitely tamed me," said a very happy Isobella.

After dining at the restaurant, they returned to their tree-top cabin. It had been a very eventful day. Isobella wanted to make Michael feel special. He picked her up and carried her to bed, then he started to undress. As Isobella was lying in the four-poster she had a vision of Mason; she reached up and pulled Michael down on to her, she was in a frenzy, she tried to rip the rest of the clothes off his body. She slid out of her dress and kicked her knickers off and held him close so she could feel the heat off his body and his manly parts near hers. She wanted him so badly. "Please take me now," she whispered. This Michael wanted to hear from his beloved Isobella, and they bathed in the pleasure of each other's bodies, remembering that today they had made a vow that would bind them together for many years to come.

This was how they woke the next morning. Michael had never been so happy, Isobella was his at last. He wanted to stay high up in the tree-tops with her forever. They decided that they would stay another night so it was arranged, and Michael went back to bed and cuddled up to Isobella where they spent most of the day. She felt a little ashamed about last night as she thought it was Mason in her arms, that was why she became the lioness attacking its prey. Michael was still a learner. Isobella had to be careful, as she did not want to hurt his feelings or feel she was taking control away him.

The honeymoon was over, and they were nearly home. As they drove down Parity Lane and neared their home, Isobella saw a powder-blue Ferrari parked in their driveway. "Michael, what a beautiful car," she said. "This is my wedding present to you, it is in your name, it belongs to you." Isobella was ecstatic; she did dream one day she would be driving a Lamborghini, but here she was with her own Ferrari, and powder blue, of all colours. She remembered Laura turning up at Jannie and Mason's wedding in a powder-blue Ferrari and she was so jealous, now she had the latest model, and it was her very own. "Michael, I don't know what to say, you are a wonderful man, I promise to look after you," she sobbed with happiness. She clung to him, she saw him as a father figure and she wanted to protect him.

Life was back to normal, Michael had returned to work

and Isobella was at the Guccia store. Natalie told Isobella that a man had been in several times asking for her but she would give out no information. "I think it was the man you modelled the dresses for and he asked for your address. He seemed pretty keen to speak to you," she said. "That would be right, Natalie, I nearly killed him. He came to my house and attacked me, so I clobbered him with my standard lamp, then I had to call the ambulance. Please don't tell anybody, Michael doesn't even know." "Oh, I'm sorry, Isobella, was that because I gave him your address?" asked Natalie. "Don't worry, he won't bother me any more, now that I'm married to Michael," replied Isobella.

Later in the week Toby came into the store to speak with Isobella. He couldn't look her in the eye, he was so ashamed of his behaviour at her home that night. "I'm so embarrassed, in fact I'm more than that, I'm ashamed of myself, I'm sorry, Isobella. I want to apologise to you and Michael." "It's only me you have to apologise to, Michael knows nothing of this, I haven't mentioned it to him," replied Isobella curtly, "but put a foot wrong and he will know." This was a huge load off his shoulders as he had been living in fear of losing his job with his company, because of Michael being their number one investor. "Michael and I are married, just so that you know," she said. Toby couldn't get out of the store quick enough, he was so relieved that this would go no further; all he had to do now was control his feelings for Isobella.

Laura came around to see Michael one weekend, and it ended in tears. She thought a reconciliation might have been possible, but when she learnt that he and Isobella were married, she was in total shock. Now that Isobella was living in her home, and driving the latest model Ferrari, it was just too much for her; she left the home crying her heart out, as it was all too late. She would never get Michael back now. She wanted to tell him about Isobella and Mason, but she couldn't afford to lose any more friendships.

Laura went home and rung Lillian to tell her Michael had remarried. When she told Lillian that he had married Isobella, the phone went dead. She couldn't believe what Laura was telling her. Still no one knew the connection between Isobella and James. Everyone apart from Natalie blamed Michael for the marriage break-up, and Laura didn't want it to be any other way. As long as she was in the clear and Jannie didn't find out, then that was fine.

That night Lillian broke the news to James about Michael and Isobella. He was in total disbelief! He liked Michael, he found him a sensible high-powered business-man, and a rich one at that, but down to earth. Fancy Isobella having won Michael's heart; this was a bit hard for James to digest as he thought Michael would have seen right through Isobella. But he had no knowledge of her changed behaviour.

It was only one month to go before Michael and Isobella's pilgrimage to 'their' little church for their first wedding anniversary. Michael was still very much in love with Isobella and she had accompanied him to several more Grands Prix and other car-racing events during that time. He loved that she took the time to be with him, because this was Laura's downfall. He had been to his solicitors and changed his will, leaving Isobella the home and his superannuation payout. The rest of his assets were left 50/50 to Mathew and Isobella. He had discussed some of his holdings with Isobella, so she knew he owned two blocks of upmarket townhouses, as he was the developer and owner. They were let out to company representatives so had reliable tenants. No one really knew Michael's wealth as he never talked about it. One day he would explain it all to Isobella.

She loved her powder-blue Ferrari. She had parked her own car in the garage at her home, as it was made redundant. She drove her Ferrari to work every morning and loved the attention it drew. One day Jannie called into the store and asked Isobella if she would ask Michael to come and see her at the weekend. She agreed to let Michael know.

Isobella had only caught glances of Mason in the last few months, but last Friday she saw him coming towards her in the blood-red Lamborghini; he signalled for her to stop, but she knew it would be fatal so just kept driving. No way would she hurt Michael, she had forsaken her own desires, sometimes fantasising with Michael that she was with Mason, this was when she enjoyed her lovemaking most.

Michael received a phone call from Mathew, who was most upset as he hadn't been told about his father remarrying. He heard it from his mother. This was an oversight on Michael's behalf so he apologised to his son, but he was an adult, not a child. Mathew wanted to know all about his father's new wife, and when he mentioned about her being there for his wealth, this was the very wrong thing to say to Michael. He was the one that pursued Isobella, not the other way around, and he let Mathew know this. Other people had the same impression, namely James and Lillian, but Michael was very happy so that was all that mattered.

The following weekend Michael mentioned to Isobella that he was going to see Jannie, did she want to come? Isobella said she thought that perhaps Jannie wanted to talk business, so she would stay at home. Michael came over and took her in his arms and told her how much he loved her and kissed her on the cheek. "I will be back soon," he said. They had planned to go over their plans for their trip away in three weeks' time. He drove out to Lauderdale Street then down the tree-lined driveway to the mansion. He saw Mason out in the garden and called to him. "Is Jannie home?" "What do you want with Jannie?" he answered. Michael was upset about this as it was none of his business. "This is between Jannie and me," was all he said. Mason panicked as he thought Michael was going to spill the beans on him and Laura. And besides, he could not see Isobella as long as she was with him. He was so angry he let fly with his fist and landed a blow to Michael's head, knocking him to the ground. He lay there for a few minutes, then picked himself up and stumbled to his car. He climbed in and sat for a moment, then started the car. He drove down the driveway and into Lauderdale street, and only made it halfway down when he pulled over and slumped behind the wheel.

A passing motorist saw Michael in this position so rang for an ambulance. He looked in the car but couldn't see if he was still breathing. He waited there until the ambulance arrived. The medics applied oxygen to Michael and took him away to hospital.

Isobella received a phone call asking her to come to the hospital as her husband was in intensive care. What had happened to Michael? She panicked. When she arrived at the hospital she was shown straight to his room. He was hooked up to machines, she ran to him and squeezed his hand and held it tight. The doctors were trying to find out what had happened to him, as he had bruises and damage in the head area, but he hadn't crashed the car, he had just slumped over the steering wheel, which would not have caused these wounds. They asked Isobella where he had been and she told them he was going to see a friend in Lauderdale Street. Yes, that was the area where he was found in his car. Michael opened his eyes to see his beloved Isobella there with him, he smiled then closed his eyes and went to sleep, never to wake. Isobella was brokenhearted, her father figure had been taken from her. She was still holding his hand. The tears flowed, as he was never going to make it to 'their' church again, the one thing he was so looking forward to.

She didn't know what to do, so she rang Natalie. Natalie came straight to the hospital to be with Isobella to comfort her. She sat there sobbing. What had happened to Michael? No one had said what was wrong. With that, the doctor came out and asked Isobella some questions. "Did your husband have a fall today or yesterday? We found bruising and signs of head injuries relating to a fall or being hit. Can you explain how this may have happened to him?" "No, he was fine this morning, he kissed me before he left to go to Lauderdale Street, and said he would be back soon," sobbed Isobella. "That's where he was found, slumped over the wheel of his car halfway down Lauderdale Street. He was on his way back; who had he been to visit?" asked the doctor. They were trying to shed some light on what had gone wrong. The doctor asked Isobella to ring her friend to see if he was okay when he left them. With this she rung Jannie, but Mason answered the phone. "Mason, did Michael come to your home this morning?" she sobbed. "What is wrong, has something happened?" "Yes, Michael has passed away, he was found in his car in your street," said a teary Isobella. Mason's heart sank; was it the punch he landed that had killed Michael? "Did you see him this morning?" Isobella asked again. Mason had to think quickly, no way did he want a finger pointed at him, in case there was an inquiry. He said he hadn't seen Michael and neither had Jannie, as she was away in town.

The doctor said there would be a postmortem as they had to try to establish a cause for Michael's death. "I'll have to report this to the police, so they will call and ask you questions." Natalie wanted to drive Isobella home, but she wanted to be on her own, as she couldn't bring herself to believe Michael was gone, and she would have to ring Mathew. She asked Natalie to ring Laura and tell her about Michael.

Mathew was shocked to hear that his father had passed away. He wanted to know what happened, but Isobella could only tell him what she knew. Until the postmortem was held, they would just have to wait. He told Isobella he would fly out from Shanghai as soon as he could. She offered for him to stay at their home, but he said he would stay with his mother. They had never met, and he still wondered if it was his father's wealth that had attracted her in the first place.

Natalie rang Laura to tell her what had happened. Laura was in shock and broke down as she still had feelings for Michael. He had provided well for her over the years, and she was the one who had done him wrong. Laura contacted Mathew, who had been speaking to Isobella; he was still in shock. In turn she rang Lillian and Jannie to let them know about Michael.

Isobella lay on the bed and cried her heart out; in only three weeks they going to celebrate their first anniversary. Now she had no Michael. She thought about how determined he was to get back to 'their' church. 'I will take you back, Michael, we will have your service at our church', she made a promise to herself. He would love that, to visit one last time. What of her life now? She closed her eyes, and suddenly a silhouette appeared: it was Tilly Dunnage. Was this the sadness she predicted? But Isobella thought it was Matilda, not yet fully realising that her reading only related to the future.

# 12

# Life after Michael

Isobella was disturbed by a knock on the door. She was a mess, as she had not stopped crying. Who could that be? she wondered. She went to the door and there were two policemen standing there. They asked if they could come in and speak to her. "We are sorry to hear about your husband, but we have to try and establish what happened. His injuries are not consistent with how he was found in his car. Was he in good health when he left here?" Isobella told them exactly what she had told the doctor, that Michael was just going to visit a friend, then he was coming back home. They could see she was distraught, so said they would leave her, but they may have to come back. As the police were leaving, Jannie and Mason arrived.

Jannie came up to Isobella and gave her a hug. "Oh Isobella, I'm so sorry, I really liked Michael, he was a dear friend. Tell me what happened." "Michael went to see you, but he didn't make it home; he was found in Lauderdale Street slumped over the steering wheel, he was on his way home," she sobbed. "What were the police doing here?" Jannie asked. "They were trying to establish what happened, as Michael had head injuries, but they were not related to his accident," answered Isobella.

When Mason heard this, he felt sick. He had only wanted to scare Michael, not kill him.

The way was now clear for Mason. With Michael gone there would be no one to tell Jannie about his and Laura's affair. But this was not so; Isobella had witnessed that night, but no one knew she was there. She had told Natalie about the affair so as to take the blame of the marriage break-up away from Michael. Mason missed Isobella, Jannie had become boring, and if need be, he would leave Jannie because Isobella was now a very rich sexy lady. He could have it all.

Isobella had to ring the Ferrari company to let them know Michael had passed away. Because he was the CEO he was his own boss, so she contacted his secretary. When she heard about Michael she burst into tears, and promised to let the head of the company know. Everyone would miss him at Ferrari headquarters.

Mathew had arrived from Shanghai, so Laura brought him around to meet Isobella. Any bad feelings between Laura and Isobella had to be put aside until this was all over. He looked very much like his father but didn't have his warmth or personality. They had lots of things to discuss. Laura wanted to know what was happening about Michael's funeral. Isobella knew exactly what was going to happen, she was taking him back to 'their' church for his last visit. "The service is going to be held in a little church in Laidley, where we were married. Michael and I planned to go back," then she stopped as the tears flowed.

"He will be buried back here." "What about his possessions?" asked Mathew. "You are most welcome to take what you want, Mathew, your father would want you to have them," she said. "Just give me a couple of days and I will sort them out for you. Michael's solicitor has asked that we all be at his office in Hamilton Street at 10.30am tomorrow for the reading of his will."

The next morning, they assembled at the solicitor's office as requested. He asked them to be seated. Isobella had no idea what was in the will, as they had never discussed it. 'To my Isobella I bequeath our home, my superannuation fund and any other monies in my bank accounts. The rest of my estate I leave 50/50 to Isobella and Mathew.' Laura never got a mention; she was in disbelief, as she thought with all Michael's wealth, he would have provided for her. Even Mathew was dumbfounded that there was nothing for his mother. "Why would Dad do this to my mother?" asked Mathew. "He only knew Isobella for a year, why should she get most of the money?" "Your father loved Isobella dearly, he had never been so happy, he told me this when he changed his will," said the solicitor. "He said Laura would understand why she got nothing. I don't know what this means, but apparently Laura knows." Mathew looked at Isobella with distaste; he would fight this case in court, his mother deserved some of the money. He was well equipped to handle this situation as he was a high-flying lawyer with a big law company overseas. "The total worth of Michael's estate is $97 million. I will have to proportion this to Michael's wishes. This will take me a couple of weeks, then we will have another meeting. Both you, Isobella and Mathew, are trustees to Michael's will. Until our next meeting, thank you," said the solicitor. Isobella could not believe Michael was worth that amount of money. She had not thought about money while she was with him, she knew he was rich, but not how rich. She looked upon him as a father figure, he was her protector. "I will tell you now, Isobella, I'm going to fight this in court, my mother is entitled to my father's money and I will see she gets it," said Mathew. "Your father chose me, Mathew, I didn't make the first move, he loved me. I can understand why you are angry, but these are his wishes, not mine," replied Isobella. "Just come around when you are ready and pick up anything of your father's that you want."

Isobella had asked Natalie for the week off work. She went home and sat out on the balcony trying to put things into perspective. Her thoughts drifted back to Tilly Dunnage. She predicted sadness and wealth; how did she know this was going to happen? She could have warned Isobella that Michael was going to die, she would have gone with him to Jannie's that day, then perhaps this would not have happened. Things were flying around in her head, when suddenly she realised that what Tilly predicted was indeed in the future after all. It was her, not Tilly, that had mixed the past with the future.

Michael's body had still not been released to his family, as the cause of death had not been established. All his organs were perfect, so it now came down to the blow on the head. But how did this happen? The police came back to Isobella just to be reassured that Michael had not had a fall. His wallet and money were still in his pocket so no one had robbed him. They decided they would call on the public for help. They would put a notice in the local paper asking anyone who had been to the Lauderdale Reserve on

17th April between the hours of 10.30am and 12.30pm to please contact them.

Isobella had contacted the marriage celebrant that had married them and told her of Michael's death. She remembered them because of the flowers they donated to the hospital. Isobella asked if she could hold Michael's service at the church, and would she officiate. She agreed, and Isobella was to let her know as soon as his body was given back to her.

Today was Michael's funeral. Many people had gathered at the little church to say their final farewells. Representatives from the Ferrari company came, they respected Michael immensely as he had been with them right from the start of his working life. He would be sorely missed. At one stage, she saw James and Lillian in the background, but they would keep well away from her; she also spotted Toby, the real-estate agent. Isobella had written a little speech she wanted to read out at the service. "This is the little church Michael and I chose to be married in. We made a promise to each other we would return every year to celebrate our wedding anniversaries. Sadly, we are one week early, but not to celebrate our anniversary, but to celebrate Michael's life. He would have loved this, he so wanted to come back to our church, that is why we are here today." Then the tears started; this was all she could manage as she was overcome with grief.

Before she left, the head man of Ferrari who had flown in for the day for Michael's funeral came up to Isobella and slipped her an envelope. "This we would like you to have, Michael was a dedicated man to his work and his company, we all respected him and will miss him. Please keep coming to the racing circuits, we will send you passes to attend any functions that we run. I am truly sorry, Isobella." When she had time to look in the envelope there was a cheque for $250,000. She wept, to think that he was worth all this money, now that he was gone. Isobella was back at work, she found the nights lonely at home without Michael. Laura and Mathew were building a case against her. Mathew had to give up his position as trustee to contest the will. Laura was a woman scorned, Mason wanted nothing to do with her, for fear of Jannie finding out, and now she had lost Michael. He had left her out of his will. She had received a payment when they separated, but with all his wealth, she thought she was entitled to much more.

It was just over a month since Michael had passed away. Mason was hanging out to make contact with Isobella. His life with Jannie had changed so much and his feelings for her were dwindling. He longed for Isobella's hot lovemaking, it was driving him mad, so he drove around to her house one night and knocked on her door. Isobella opened the door and there stood Mason. She didn't know what to do, she went weak at the knees and her heart started pounding. This was still the man that messed with her heart. He let himself in and closed the door. He picked her up and carried her over to the sheepskin rug that was on the lounge floor and lay her down. He knelt down and started to undress her, he wanted to feel her naked body close to his. It was a long time since he had been sexually aroused, and it didn't take long for the passion to ignite between them. The lioness was on the prowl, she had her prey, now she would devour it. This is what Mason loved about Isobella, she was exciting, tantalising, and knew how to make a man happy. Oh, how he missed this playful love.

Isobella lay there, it had all happened before she realised. Mason had that effect on her, she just melted, then she became so aroused she would lose control. No man had ever come close to Mason, he made her feel alive. He was not half the man as such that Michael was, but he lit a fire within her that she couldn't put out. It just kept smouldering away.

Mason let himself out and closed the door. Isobella lay on the sheepskin for ages thinking about him, and to think he was back in her life, made her very happy. But hovering above her was the ghost of Michael holding his arms out for her. She turned over and tried to bury her head in the sheepskin, hoping he would go away, but he wouldn't leave her. It was as if he was trying to lift her up and take her with him. She lay there sobbing; was it guilt or was it happiness? Was this who would haunt her from the past? Tilly had predicted that she would be haunted by a person from the past. It wasn't Matilda at all, it was Michael. How did she know this?

Isobella took an early lunch leave from the store as she had a meeting with Michael's solicitor at 11.30am. He told her that Mathew and Laura were putting together a case for a larger share of Michael's estate. "But Michael left it the way he wanted it," said Isobella. "Yes, you know that, and I know that, but it can be challenged in court," he explained. "They will try to come at us with all the dirt they can get, just so as you know this." If Isobella's memory served her correctly, did she not remember that Matilda's will was left 50/50 but she challenged it, and the judge rendered the will invalid in her favour. But she had a short memory very much like Matilda's, only remembering what she wanted to. Thank goodness Michael had a happy year with Isobella, and that his father figure had a calming influence over her.

No one knew anything about her past except James

and Lillian, but James would never want to be associated with her, for all the heartache she had put them through.

Isobella was worried; should she pay Tilly Dunnage another visit, just to see if she could shed some light on what she might expect in the future?

She retraced her steps she had taken that night, and ended up in the park. She must have passed Tilly's without seeing it, so she walked back. She found the alleyway but no booth and no signage. She went into the shop at the start of the alleyway and inquired about Tilly. "Oh, one day someone went in to have their future told and found Tilly slumped over her crystal ball. She was dead. No one knew how long she had been there. The dear old soul, I wonder if she had family. They just came and took her away in the hearse, she's probably buried in a pauper's grave. What a strange name she had. The story goes she arrived here one day and set up her booth. She sat there every day for the fifteen years that I have been here, probably been here many more years before that. I took her sign down and put it my storeroom. The council came and dismantled her booth and threw it on the back of the rubbish truck," the shopkeeper told her. "Could I please buy her sign off you?" asked Isobella. "Good lord, lady, you don't have to buy it, you can take it. Just a minute until I find it," he said. The man came out with Tilly's sign; it was covered in cobwebs and dust.

"Just a minute, I will brush all the shit off it," he said. As he handed her the sign a cold chill went down her spine,; she remembered this feeling the day Tilly took her hand and led her into her booth. Isobella insisted the shopkeeper take a $50 note, the sign had to be worth something. Poor Tilly, was she the convict girl that had come out from God knows where, as Isobella had first imagined.

She put the sign under her arm and away she went. 'Oh Tilly Dunnage, whatever your life, you will never be forgotten, you dear lonely soul,' Isobella promised her.

That night Mason came to her home. Isobella told him the story of Tilly Dunnage, but did not disclose any thing about her reading. She showed him the sign, she had polished it, and now it had pride of place in her home. She was sure Tilly would have been happy, that her name was in someone's care. "Whatever happens I will find your resting place one day, Tilly, I promise," swore Isobella.

It didn't take long before the passionate lovemaking started. But while this was happening, another happening was taking place outside Isobella's home. Laura had come to talk to Isobella and saw the blood-red Lamborghini parked in the driveway. She fumbled in the glovebox and got her camera out and took a photo, and made sure the date was on it. What a bitch, now I have got some dirt on her, Laura mused.

The police had several calls in relation to the Lauderdale Reserve inquiry in the paper. One was of particular interest. A lady had been walking her dog when he broke loose and ran to the reserve fence, and started barking at two men standing at the end of the lane near the big home. She distracted her dog and carried on into reserve. That was all she remembered; although it was of little significance to her, it was pivotal to the police inquiry. Now they knew there were two men there. Was it Michael and Mason? But Mason had denied seeing Michael that day; did he have something to hide?

The police now had a lead. Before this they were becoming increasingly frustrated as they knew Michael's death had nothing to do with the way he was found in his car. Had there been words between these two men? Now it was time for them to approach Mason again. They drove to Lauderdale Street then down the tree-lined driveway to the mansion. Jannie was out in the garden. They called out to her and asked if Mason was at home. She asked them to come inside, and called to him. When Mason came into the dining room and saw the police he was in shock. "We are here to ask you again, did you see Michael the morning he came to your home?" they asked. "I have already told you, I didn't see him," replied Mason. "We have evidence to the contrary. A witness saw two men talking out on the driveway around 11.00am. We think that may have been you and Michael. We will do an identity parade back at the station, unless you tell us what really happened that morning," the police asked. With this he knew he was caught, so Mason told the police they had a confrontation and he punched Michael. He didn't intentionally mean to hurt him, but because he seemed okay and drove away, he never gave it another thought. "Why didn't you tell us the truth when we first asked you?" questioned the police. Mason explained he freaked out when he heard of Michael's death, then panicked. Jannie had sat listening to this, then burst into tears. "Why did you hurt Michael, Mason, why?" she sobbed. With this the police asked Mason to accompany them to the police station for further questioning.

Jannie was brokenhearted; why had Mason hit Michael? She could see no reason for this, he wasn't a violent man, neither of them were. She desperately needed someone to talk to and the nearest friend was Natalie. She climbed into the Lamborghini and drove to the Guccia store. As she walked into the store she was still crying and she asked Isobella if Natalie was there. When Natalie saw her, she led her into her office and made her sit down, then she shut the door. Isobella was in a panic; had Jannie been told about her and Mason?

"Jannie, what has happened?" asked Natalie. Jannie told her what had happened and now Mason was at the police station being questioned. Natalie didn't know what to say to Jannie, as she knew about the affair between Mason and Laura. Isobella had told her but she couldn't say anything to her because she was sworn to secrecy, and now was not the right time. Jannie needed all the comforting she could get. "Isobella, could you look after the store, I'm going home with Jannie," said Natalie. She wanted to be with her until Mason came home. "What would make Mason hit Michael? If they find out this was the cause of his death, he will be had up for manslaughter, or worse murder," Jannie said sobbing inconsolably. "He is a good man." Natalie could tell her different, but not now; it would all come out, and it would be the end of a schoolgirl friendship that had spanned many years. So many secrets were about to be revealed.

Mason arrived home in the police car. The police came in and told Jannie that they would be back tomorrow morning to take him in for further questioning, then they left. "Please, Mason, tell me why you hit Michael, I can't understand why you would do this," begged Jannie. "I asked him to come around to see me, as I had business I wanted to discuss with him." Mason couldn't believe he just heard this; so all Michael wanted was to see Jannie on business, not to expose him. He was furious, why didn't she say he was coming around? Now he was in serious trouble; for what? For nothing. He was blown away, this didn't need to happen; if only he could go back in time, but it was too late.

Isobella was exciting and he couldn't wait to see her

again, but this was not going to be a happening thing. Mason and Isobella were two of a kind, they lived for their own pleasures without a thought to whom they may hurt. "I'm sorry, Jannie, I didn't mean to hurt Michael. I panicked when I heard he had died, now I'm in big trouble with the police," said a sad Mason. Natalie was a silent witness to all this, she just wished that scumbag Mason would come clean to Jannie, but she was going to find the truth the hard way.

When Natalie arrived back at the store, Isobella was still there. She had waited, as she wondered what was wrong with Jannie. Natalie had to be careful how she handled this, because Isobella was going to be terribly upset. "Sit down, Isobella. I have something to tell you, it is going to make you very angry. That morning that Michael went to Jannie's, Mason punched him in the head and the police think that was the cause of Michael's death. They took Mason in for questioning, and are coming to take him back into custody tomorrow morning." Isobella went into meltdown. She could not believe what she had just heard. Mason was responsible for Michael's death and she had been sleeping with him in Michael's home. She ran to the toilet and threw up. Her lover was responsible for her husband's death, how bizarre was that, what the hell was Mason thinking? She broke down and cried her heart out. Natalie went to put her arms around her, but Isobella stood up, she just wanted to go home, to be on her own.

Isobella didn't know how she drove home, her head was all over the place. She unlocked her door and as she walked into the lounge the first thing she spotted was the sheepskin rug on the floor. She picked it up and took it outside to the rubbish bin and threw it in. Then the questions started. Why did Mason do this to Michael? Was it because he knew he couldn't have her as long as she was Michael's wife? Was she ultimately the cause of her husband's death.? So many questions and none of them made sense. She had been making love to a murderer just to satisfy her own needs. She was no better than Mason. She was still the spoilt princess who put herself first and foremost, in fact she had turned into a wicked witch still hurting others, just as she had done all her life. Her love for Mason turned to hate, but it was herself she hated.

Isobella decided once she got Michael's money she would sell up and move away, and start a new life. She would be an extremely rich heiress, the world would be her oyster. She could start her own fashion store in another city where no one knew her. She could forget James and Lillian forever, they would be history. The past wouldn't mean anything to her, in fact they would be just another name from another life.

It had now been established that Michael's death was the result of a blow to the head. All Jannie's friends and acquaintances now knew about Mason, as he was held on remand. James and Lillian didn't take long to work out why this had all happened, as they knew Isobella's background, but they kept it to themselves. Mason was being held until he came up for sentencing,so he wasn't going to get see his playful lover for a very long time.

The job at the Guccia store had lost all its excitement for Isobella, she was ready to move on. She would tell Natalie that she was going to leave before Natalie found out about her and Mason, as there would be no position there for her, once this had happened. Natalie would hate her for messing with Jannie's man. Not that anyone would want him now, he was out in the cold. As she lay on the settee alone, she picked up Tilly's sign and held it close to her heart and talked to it. "Everything is starting to make sense, dear Tilly, how did you know that what I wanted most in life, I could never have? Mason will spend years in prison, I will never find such love again. What will become of my life? You can't tell me any more, but whatever happens, you will be with me always."

Isobella had broken the news to Natalie that she was leaving. Natalie was upset but she understood why, it must be hard for her, especially with Michael gone and the court case over Michael's estate. But this was not the real reason she was leaving. Natalie was yet to learn of Mason and Isobella's affair. "Take time out, think about things, and come back when you are ready, there will always be a position here for you," Natalie told her.

Today was a big day, it was the start of the Family Court hearing over Michael's estate. Mathew and Laura were contesting the will. Mathew was a defence lawyer so he was right up there with the play. As Isobella looked around the courtroom she saw James and Lillian; what the hell are they doing here? she asked herself. It certainly wasn't to support her.

The judge called Mathew to the stand first, to put forward his case. He told the court that his mother had looked after his father for many years supporting him throughout his working life. That she was left out of his will was hurtful, and he felt she was far more deserving of the money than Isobella, who had only known his father for one year. His mother had given Michael a son, himself, and had been loyal to him all those years. That was his case put forward. Next called was Laura. She told the court that it was only one year since she and Michael separated, and that she had received a settlement payment, but it was not enough for her to live a comfortable life. Isobella had only known Michael for a year and had been left the bulk of Michael's wealth. She didn't think this was fair on herself and Mathew. Another recent happening had occurred: Michael had died as a result of a blow to the head, and this blow was delivered by Isobella's lover, Mason Rockford. Laura had taken photos, with dates, of Mason's blood-red Lamborghini parked in Isobella's driveway, only a month after Michael's death. Then she concluded, "That is all, your honour."

Isobella did not see this coming, she was dumbfounded; she had been exposed before the judge, and in front of James and Lillian. Right, this was revenge waiting to happen; if Laura could give out dirt, so would she. She started jotting down all Laura's dirty washing; it was going to be hung out and aired in this courtroom. There would be some red faces. The judge called for the court to be adjourned until tomorrow morning at 10.30am.

That night Jannie rung Lillian to talk about Mason. Lillian was heartbroken for Jannie, as she had been through enough with her first husband's death and now this. She could not bring herself to tell her what had happened at the court today, that Mason was having an affair with Isobella. This would have just been too much for her to bear. Jannie said she was going to the court tomorrow to support Laura, would they meet her there? Lillian tried to put her off, but she insisted on going. What was she going to hear tomorrow? Was this going to cement the friendship of three old school friends, Jannie, Laura and Lillian, or was the friendship going to be destroyed?

The court was in session. The judge called Isobella to the bench to put her case forward. She took a deep breath then looked around the court, and to her horror there was Jannie sitting with James and Lillian. She closed her eyes and all she could see was Michael's ghost. She felt a chill go down her spine; was Tilly here with her also? Suddenly her blood was running hot through her veins, she was here to do battle and that she would do. It was self-mode now, no one else mattered, she was doing battle for her own survival. Isobella started by telling the judge that Michael loved her, and that they had been extremely happy in their short time together. Michael had made the first move towards her, and their friendship grew from there. The reason that Michael and Laura separated was because he told her to leave when he found Laura and Mason Rockford in the Plaza Hotel together. They were having an affair, and Michael was disgusted that his wife was cheating on her best friend, he felt it was a betrayal of a long-lasting friendship. With this a loud sob rang out from the courtroom. Isobella continued. Laura spent the night before Jannie and Mason's wedding with him at the Plaza Hotel. "That's not true!" yelled Laura. "I know it is true, Laura, because I let your tyre down, that's why you couldn't drive your black Ferrari to the wedding the next day." "Don't listen to her!" Laura yelled again. The judge ordered Laura to remain silent, or she would be removed from the court, and asked Isobella to continue with her case. "Michael was a lonely man. Laura never accompanied him on any of his work-related assignments, he always went alone. That is why we were so happy, I went to the racing circuits with him. He needed company and I supplied that for him. Michael was a gentleman and was well respected. That is all, your honour."

The judge stood up and said court would resume at 1.30pm. As Isobella got down from the stand and walked out of the courtroom, she ran into Laura. "You dirty little schemer, look what you have done to Jannie, she is inconsolable. I hope you get nothing from Michael's estate," she threatened Isobella. "If you can play dirty, so can I. We have both lost Michael and Mason, but imagine what Jannie and Lillian will think of you," Isobella retaliated. "They will hate you, you have more to lose than me." With that she tossed her head in the air and walked to her car, as she didn't want to have to face Jannie or Lillian and James. The sooner this was over, the better; she could move on and start all over again with her new-found riches.

James and Lillian were left to console Jannie; this was a terrible shock for her, first Mason and now Laura. How could Laura do such a thing to an old friend, and Mason, just as well he was in custody, otherwise she might have killed him. It was now starting to come together, and her mind flashed back to the day Isobella came to the mansion and asked her who owned the property and the Lamborghini. Was she mixed up in this too? she asked Lillian. Because she had not attended yesterday's court, she didn't know Isobella was also Mason's lover. Lillian had to tell Jannie what happened yesterday and this just added to her misery.

The court resumed at 1.30pm. The judge started her cross-examination, beginning with Laura. "Is what Isobella said about an affair with this Mason true?" "Yes, your honour, deep down I loved Michael but he never had time for me, his work always came first," she replied. "I think if you had been a better companion to him he might not have looked elsewhere for comfort. Why do you think you are entitled to more of the estate money?" questioned the judge. "Michael and I have been together most of our lives, we had Mathew our son, he was our only child. Because Isobella only knew Michael for a year, it shouldn't entitle her to most of his estate," Laura answered. "Thank you, stand down," said the judge.

Then she called Isobella to the stand. She could see why any man would be proud to have her hanging from his arm, she was one good-looking lady. "Did you know this Mason before you met Michael? Were you lovers? "Yes, we were," she replied. With this she heard Jannie sobbing. "Were you lovers while you were married to Michael?" the judge asked. "No, I was true to Michael." "But you resumed your affair soon after Michael's death. I have photos of a red Lamborghini parked in your driveway. Is this his car?" and she held up the photos.

"Yes, your honour," answered Isobella. "Please stand down," said the judge. She had heard enough.

"This is a tangled web, and I am deeply sorry that Michael was caught up in it. He deserved better, he seemed to be an upstanding man, and extremely wealthy. Do you know the heartache you both have brought to the people around you? The court will adjourn for today, I will make my decision tomorrow. Court will resume at 10.30am in the morning." The judge had spoken.

James and Lillian were the only two people in the courtroom that knew what Isobella was capable of. This was a replica of Matilda's estate, but now she was the one being challenged. They hoped that the ruling would go against her, this would-be karma. It would be good for her to experience what it was like to be on the losing side of life. Meanwhile they had to help Jannie through all this, as now she knew Mason had two lovers, both people she knew. She was utterly destroyed.

Now that Jannie had heard how Isobella fitted into the picture, her thoughts on her right from the start were coming to bear. "I always wondered about Isobella, what a horrible person she is." James felt devastated, as once again his sister Isobella had left shambles in her wake. If only Bartholomew and Matilda had known what a wicked person their daughter turned out to be. She was like a hurricane; she blew in and caused havoc, then left devastation in her wake.

Meanwhile Mathew couldn't believe what he had just heard about his mother; he felt betrayed. That she had an affair with Aunty Jannie's new husband was unforgivable. Now he understood why his parents had separated, as his father would not have stood for Jannie being hurt, as she was a dear friend. This shed a different light on things; perhaps the settlement payout his mother had received was all his father thought Laura deserved. Mathew was hurt deeply to learn this today about his mother; the sooner it was all settled, then he could return to Shanghai. He had some soul-searching to do. Did his mother deserve any more of Michael's estate? Was this her punishment?

Today was judgment day. Everyone assembled at the court. Isobella held her head high, whereas Laura hung hers in shame, as she had no friends left. The judge arrived, and asked Mathew, Laura and Isobella to come to the bench. "In summing up this case, there has been a lot of deceit exposed in this courtroom, and a lot of people have been hurt. Michael's estate is very large, but that does not excuse the behaviour of these two women, namely Isobella and Laura, who have both lost two men in their lives, but who did not appreciate the man whose estate we are talking about today. For this reason I have revoked Michael's will and awarded as follows: to Laura $1 million; to Isobella the home and $1 million; to Mathew the balance of the estate."

Isobella's wealth was gone, this was just a mere pittance to what she had been left by Michael. His estate was worth $97 million and all she ended up with was $1 million.

Isobella could not understand how this could happen as Michael's wishes had not been followed, and she was the one that should have received the bulk of his money, as it was left to her. She deserved it. Where was the justice in this? she asked herself. Where would she go from here, as now she was not the rich heiress that she thought she was going to be. Her dreams were shattered.

Did she not remember a few years back, to when her brother James was left fifty percent of their family wealth, but someone took it from him, namely Isobella? Suddenly a cold shiver went down her spine; Tilly's last prediction was about to be delivered. From the silence of the courtroom a voice rang out: "Justice has been done." Isobella looked around to see who this voice belonged to, and there, standing tall, was her brother James with a smile that said it all.

# About the
# Author

Margaret Nyhon lives in Alexandra, in the Central Otago province of New Zealand, where she writes, paints and practises the crafts of printing and bookbinding. She has worked extensively in hospitality management in New Zealand and resort management in Australia. The urge to trace her family history led to her most recent venture, the writing of her first non-fiction work, *de Marisco*. Margaret is married and has three adult children and two grandsons.

Don't miss the sequel to *Isobella*
*Isobella: Self Redemption* — Coming Soon!

# Acknowledgements

To my family for their contributions and their patience while I was absorbed in writing my novel.

To Kath and Kathryn for their helpful comments.

To my grandson in helping with the cover design.

To Eva for her proofreading.

To Martin who assisted me in the publication.